THE RANDOM HOUSE BOOK OF
GREEK MYTHS

THE RANDOM HOUSE BOOK OF
GREEK MYTHS

By Joan D. Vinge
ILLUSTRATED BY Oren Sherman

RANDOM HOUSE
NEW YORK

For Jessi and Josh, with love
—J.D.V.

For Rick
—O.S.

Text copyright © 1999 by Joan D. Vinge. Illustrations copyright © 1999 by Oren Sherman. All rights reserved under International and Pan-American Copyright Conventions. Published in the United States by Random House, Inc., New York, and simultaneously in Canada by Random House of Canada Limited, Toronto.

www.randomhouse.com/kids

Library of Congress Cataloging-in-Publication Data
Vinge, Joan D.
The Random House book of Greek myths / by Joan D. Vinge ; illustrated by Oren Sherman.
p. cm.
Summary: Retells some of the most famous Greek myths about gods, goddesses, humans, heroes, and monsters, explaining the background of the tales and how they have survived.
ISBN 0-679-82377-8 (trade). — ISBN 0-679-92377-2 (lib. bdg.)
I. Mythology, Greek—Juvenile literature. [I. Mythology, Greek.]
I. Sherman, Oren. II. Title.
BL782.V49 1999 292.1'3—dc21 99-19080

Printed in the United States of America 10 9 8 7 6 5 4 3 2 1

RANDOM HOUSE and colophon are trademarks of Random House, Inc.

CONTENTS

INTRODUCTION

In ancient Greece, just as in our world today, things happened to people that were beyond anyone's control. Some of those things were sad and painful: earthquakes, floods, the death of loved ones. Others were happy and fortunate, but just as baffling: sudden good luck, narrow escapes, unexpected love. To make sense of those things, and to try to give meaning to their own fates, the ancient Greeks told stories.

These stories were about their gods. The Greeks believed their gods had created the heavens and the earth, and controlled the fates of human beings and all living things. The stories explained how the gods had come to be, and what they were like. Other ancient peoples also worshiped the natural elements as gods, but the Greeks imagined that their gods had lives and feelings like their own—only more so. The gods were more beautiful and much more powerful, and they lived forever. They could shower mortals who honored them with blessings or make anyone who snubbed them completely miserable. Their superhuman passions—their loves and hates and jealousies—could literally move mountains, make rivers disappear, and cause new islands to rise from the sea.

Stories about the gods—or myths—were the earliest literature and the earliest attempts to explain the natural world. But the real reason why the Greek myths are still remembered today is because they are such good stories. Down through the ages, people have enjoyed telling them again and again.

Some of the tales in this book actually began as accounts of things that had happened to the ancestors of the Greeks who wrote them down: wars, invasions, the adventurous deeds of famous heroes and heroines. Those stories also were told and retold, changing with each new storyteller, until they became legends, as colorful and strange as the stories of the gods. They are usually entangled with the gods' own adventures.

Some experts on mythology believe that in the original version of the myths, goddesses ruled the heavens and earth. By the time the myths came to be written down, centuries later, the Greeks' view of their gods had changed. In the stories you will read here, the male gods most often are the center of attention, although you will still find many goddesses who are equally brave, wise, and clever—or foolish, vain, and jealous.

In any case, it is these very human gods and goddesses whose larger-than-life adventures have kept so many people fascinated for thousands of years. I hope you will enjoy their stories, too.

IN THE BEGINNING

The ancient Greeks said that no one remembered the beginning of time, for at the beginning the earth did not exist. There was only formless Chaos. After the passing of countless years, Mother Earth—whose name was Gaia—took form out of the swirling darkness.

Mother Earth was lonely, for she had no children yet, and no one to talk to. Out of her loneliness was born Father Sky. Mother Earth looked up one night and found his dark eyes sparkling with stars, looking down at her. He smiled a new-moon smile. They fell in love.

Their newfound happiness created the plants and the animals. Mother Earth and Father Sky had many children together, as well. The first of their children were the twelve Titans. There were six sons and six daughters, and they were the first gods and goddesses.

Cronus was their leader, along with his wife, Rhea. They ruled over all the creatures of the earth. It was a golden age of peace.

But in time, Cronus began to take advantage of his power. He also began to fear that one of his children would overthrow him. So each year when his wife, Rhea, gave birth to a baby, he swallowed it. He swallowed five of his children.

Rhea was furious. When her sixth child was born, she hid the baby boy, whose name was Zeus, in a cave. Zeus grew into a handsome and powerful young man. He swore that he would save his brothers and sisters when he was old enough. One day Zeus met Metis, the daughter of another Titan. She became his first wife. She was very wise, and gave him a magic potion that helped him rescue his brothers and sisters from Cronus' belly.

Zeus and his siblings declared war on their father and his followers. After a long and terrible battle, the Titans were defeated by the new generation of gods. Zeus, his brothers, and his sisters became the rulers of the universe. They imprisoned the old gods in the dreadful pits of Tartarus, the underworld—all but Atlas, the Titans' leader in battle. Zeus forced Atlas to take the weight of the whole sky on his shoulders. He would have to hold it up until the end of time.

At last the new gods had no more enemies to fear. The world's wounds healed, and all its creatures lived in peace once again. The new family of gods began to make themselves at home.

MOUNT OLYMPUS

The gods made their home above the clouds on Mount Olympus, the highest mountain in Greece. The Cyclopes, one-eyed giants who were both smiths and skillful builders, created beautiful mansions for the gods there in the eternal sunlight. Each god and goddess had a palace, but when they attended to important questions about mortal affairs—such as who should win a war or whether they should punish some king or queen—they met in Zeus' palace, where they each had a throne.

Zeus, who controlled the lightning and thunder, sat at the head of the great hall, on a throne of polished black marble decorated with gold. Seven rainbow-colored steps led up to it.

Zeus' second wife, Queen Hera, sat next to him on an ivory throne, with three crystal steps leading up to it. She was the goddess who was the protector of women and took special care to watch over marriages and families.

Poseidon, god of the seas and rivers, sat next to his brother Zeus. Poseidon's throne was of sea-green marble, decorated with coral, gold, and polished shell.

Across from Poseidon sat their sister Demeter, the goddess of the grains and fruits people raised for food. She usually had her little daughter, Persephone, sitting on her knee. Her throne was made of spring-green malachite, which looked like waving grasses. It was decorated with golden ears of barley and small golden pigs.

Beside Poseidon sat Hephaestus, who was a son of Zeus and Hera. Hephaestus was the god of fire, of blacksmiths, and of jewelers, masons, and carpenters. He built the thrones of all the gods. His own throne was a work of art, created of all the different metals and jewels that existed. The throne could move on its own wherever Hephaestus wanted it to go.

Next to Hephaestus sat Ares, the god of war. His throne was made of brass, decorated with skulls. On its seat was a cushion made from human skin. Ares was very proud of it.

Across from Hephaestus sat his half-sister Athena, the goddess of wisdom, on a silver throne whose back was woven gold. A crown of violets made from blue lapis lazuli was set above it, and fierce monster faces were its hand rests.

Next to Athena sat Aphrodite, the goddess of love and beauty. The back of her silver, bejeweled throne was formed like a scallop shell, for she was born of sea foam.

Beside Aphrodite sat Artemis, the Lady of Wild Things. She was a daughter of Zeus and the goddess Leto, and the twin sister of the god Apollo. Artemis sat on a silver throne in the great hall. Its back was shaped like a palm tree, in memory of her mother.

Apollo, her brother, was the god of light, reason, truth, and music. He sat across the hall from Artemis on a golden throne covered with magic inscriptions.

Hermes, fleet-footed and lighthearted, sat beside Apollo. He was also a son of Zeus, and the god of shepherds, travelers, merchants, thieves, and all others who lived by their wits. Hermes' throne was made from a single piece of solid gray rock, with a symbol chiseled into its back that stood for the fire bow, a tool he had invented. Before the fire bow, people could not start a new fire without saving a glowing coal from the old one.

Zeus' sister Hestia was the goddess of the hearth, the symbol of the home, and every home in ancient Greece held a shrine to her. Hestia sat on a plain wooden throne, which was as modest in appearance as she was.

Hades, Zeus' other brother, had no throne of his own, for he was the god of the dead, and rarely left his dim, chill palace in the underworld.

One day the last of the gods arrived on Olympus. He was Dionysus, the god of wine, and his arrival caused the once-even number of seats in the hall to become thirteen. There was no room in the hall for another throne. Immediately the other gods and goddesses began to argue over where Dionysus should sit. None of them wanted to be the odd god out.

But Hestia peacefully rose from her throne and said, "Let him take my place. I will sit here in the center of the hall by the hearth and tend its sacred fire, which is my duty, after all."

The other gods fell silent, moved and humbled by Hestia's lack of vanity. She sat at the room's center ever after, on a wooden stool, reminding her often-forgetful family of how important it was to practice generosity and humility.

When Dionysus took his place among the gods in the great hall, Hephaestus redecorated Hestia's plain wooden throne for him as a welcoming present. It soon was gold-plated and decorated with bunches of amethyst grapes.

ZEUS

Zeus was the most powerful of all the gods, but he became their leader only after he and his brothers Hades and Poseidon drew straws. They wanted to decide fairly which of them would rule over all things. (They were not especially fair to their sisters, who were not given a chance to pick a straw.) Zeus got the longest straw and became the ruler of the heavens and earth. Poseidon got the next-longest straw and became the ruler of the seas. Hades got the short straw and was left with only Tartarus—the underworld. Armed with his lightning bolts, Zeus was the strongest of the gods and usually the bravest. He was not always the wisest, however. He had a bad temper, and could be selfish or impulsive. The other gods did not always like what he did, but he was their leader, so they tried to go along with his decisions. Although he was the king of the gods, even mortals sometimes laughed at his follies (but not too loudly).

 # HERA

Hera did not want to marry Zeus at first. Zeus did not seem like good husband material to her. After all, he had swallowed his first wife, the Titaness Metis.

Many years before, Zeus had heard a prophecy that Metis would give birth to a child who would be greater than he was. Like his father, Cronus, he was afraid of that. But he didn't want to lose Metis' good advice, so he thought of a plan. He told Metis they would have a contest in magic. "Let's see which of us can change into the smallest creature," he said. "You go first." Metis turned herself into a fly. Zeus caught her in his hand and swallowed her.

Hera knew about this and did not trust Zeus. She refused to marry him for three hundred years. But one spring Zeus caused a terrible thunderstorm and then turned himself into a small bird. He flew in through Hera's window, all wet and ruffled. She felt sorry for the poor bird and hugged it tenderly. Zeus immediately turned back into himself. He wooed her with such passion that she finally agreed to be his wife.

After they were married, Zeus went on wooing and marrying young and attractive women, mostly mortals. He told Hera he was doing it for the sake of humankind, because his sons from these marriages would be great heroes. He said his marriage to her was the only real one, because all his mortal wives would someday grow old and die. Hera would be his young and beautiful queen forever.

Hera did not think much of these excuses. She felt insulted and unhappy. But because Zeus always had his lightning bolts handy, she had a hard time getting back at him. She took out her anger on his other wives instead, whenever she found out about them.

When Hera discovered that Zeus was the father of the goddess Leto's unborn babies, she became very angry. When it was time for Leto to give birth, Hera asked Mother Earth to keep Leto from resting anywhere.

At last Leto came to the tiny floating island of Delos. Poseidon had just created it from the sea, and it was so new that it did not yet have a location on any map. Leto found shelter there, beneath its single palm tree.

Still she could not give birth. Hera had forbidden Ilithya, the goddess of childbirth, to go down to Leto. The other goddesses on Olympus felt so sorry for Leto that they decided to help her. They went to Hera with a beautiful necklace of amber and gold. They said it would be hers if she forgave Leto.

Hera, who felt a little guilty by now, agreed. She accepted the necklace, and Ilithya hurried down to Leto's resting place. Soon Leto's radiant twins were born: Artemis and Apollo.

POSEIDON

Zeus made the sea goddess Amphitrite marry Poseidon, after Poseidon drew the straw that made him the god of the seas. Poseidon got to take over all of Amphitrite's titles and powers; he now commanded the waters and all the creatures that lived in the oceans.

Poseidon and Amphitrite lived in the golden palace that had belonged to her father, Nereus, before he retired. It was surrounded by gardens of coral and pearls. Her forty-nine sisters, sea nymphs called the Nereids, lived there, too.

Like Zeus, Poseidon had several mortal wives. He was frequently away from home, because he enjoyed driving his chariot and four white horses across the sea. He loved horses, which reminded him of the breaking waves, and claimed to have created them. He was rather jealous of Zeus, because Zeus was his younger brother, and yet he had the most power and the best kingdom—one that was sunny and dry.

When Poseidon was at home in his palace under the waves, he spent much time brooding about being second best. When he was in a particularly bad mood, he would strike the sea with his trident, a three-pronged spear, to cause a storm. When he was feeling better, he would get into his horse-drawn chariot and drive across the waves again, calming the waters. Poseidon and Amphitrite had a son named Triton, a merman with a fish's tail like his grandfather Nereus. Triton was a wild youth who blew on a trumpet made of a conch shell and rode sea monsters.

HADES

Hades had chosen the shortest straw in the drawing with his brothers, so all that was left for him to rule was the underworld, Tartarus. Tartarus was a dark and terrible place, the land of the dead, where the sun never shone. Hades became a silent, cold, and pitiless king, to match the land he ruled. No mortals worshiped him, because they were afraid that even speaking his name would attract his unwanted attention. Not even his brothers or sisters enjoyed seeing him when he visited Olympus.

The main entrance to Tartarus was in the far west, below the setting sun. The god Hermes led those who had died down a long, dark tunnel to the River Styx. There a boatman called

Charon waited. Like most of the inhabitants of the underworld, Charon was a dour, mean-spirited sort. He would not carry a soul across the River Styx unless he was paid. If no one remembered to place a coin under the tongue of someone who had died before they were buried, the soul of that person could not cross over. Such souls had to wander the earth forever as ghosts.

Cerberus, the three-headed, dragon-tailed Hound of Hell, guarded the dark stone gates at the entrance to Tartarus. He kept the dead inside, and the living out. Once the souls of the dead had crossed over the River Styx, they were never allowed to return. They wandered forlornly through the Asphodel Fields, among strange pallid flowers, like dreamers who could never wake. The most wicked souls were punished by the Furies—three pitiless, vengeful women—in the dungeons of Hades' dark castle. Those who were the most valiant and good were sent on to a bright, beautiful land called the Elysian Fields, which lay just beyond Hades' dark realm.

DEMETER

Demeter, the goddess of grains and fruits, was also the goddess of the beautiful flowers and trees that made the world a pleasant place to live in. Demeter loved her daughter, Persephone, so much that she was truly happy only when Persephone was with her.

One day Hades made one of his rare visits to the surface of the earth, driving a black chariot drawn by four coal-black horses. In a meadow he saw Persephone. She was gathering flowers with her

A great crack opened in the earth, and he carried her down with him into its depths.

friends, and she looked as lovely as the spring day. Hades thought of how her shining beauty would brighten his cold, dark palace. He wanted her for his wife, but he knew that she would never marry him. No one wanted to be the queen of the dead. Besides, he knew her mother would never approve.

But he wanted her for his bride more than he had ever wanted anything. So he charged across the meadow in his black chariot. Persephone looked up in surprise. She saw a dark stranger bearing down on her; his face was both lordly and terrifying. He put an arm around her and swept her away. A great crack opened in the earth, and he carried her down with him into its depths.

The hills and valleys echoed her cry as the ground closed over her. Demeter, who was never far from her daughter, heard Persephone's cry. She flew like a bird over land and sea, searching for her daughter, but no one knew what had become of her. So Demeter asked the sun. "You look down on all the world," she said. "Tell me what happened to my daughter." Helios, the sun god, told her that Persephone was with Hades, in the land of the dead.

Demeter rushed back to Olympus and demanded that Zeus make Hades give back her daughter. Zeus, who wanted his grim brother to be happy for once, said he could not help her. Angry and filled with grief, Demeter left Olympus. She wandered the earth alone. Anyone who saw her saw only a bent, forlorn old woman. She had no heart for her duties as the goddess of growing things or for answering anyone's prayers. The earth suffered along with her. Grasses, flowers, and trees died. Humans and animals starved, for there was nothing to eat. The winter in Demeter's heart had spread over the entire world.

At last the other gods of Olympus realized that something had to be done. Reluctantly Zeus sent Hermes to tell Hades he must give up Persephone. When she heard the news, Persephone smiled for the first time since she had come into that terrible place. She missed the bright and beautiful world—and her mother—terribly.

Hades, on the other hand, was angry and dismayed. Though Persephone had been filled with sadness while she sat at his side, she still seemed to brighten his gloomy world like the sun.

"You are free to go back to your mother," Hermes said to Persephone, "unless you have eaten anything here."

Persephone turned pale, for if you ate the food of the land of death, it meant that you had accepted your fate and were doomed to stay there forever. Persephone had refused to eat the whole time she was in Tartarus or to drink the waters of the spring of Lethe, which brought forgetfulness to the spirits of the dead. But once, because she was desperately hungry, she had eaten four small seeds from a pomegranate. Hades knew this.

"She has eaten!" Hades said. "She must stay with me."

"It was only four seeds!" Persephone cried.

Hermes took them both back to Olympus, to the council hall. Persephone ran to her mother. Demeter threatened that she would never bring life back to the world if her daughter was taken from her again. At last Zeus proposed a compromise. Persephone could stay with her mother, in the land of the living, for most of the year. But for four months, one for each pomegranate seed, she had to rejoin Hades in the underworld.

Demeter, Persephone, and Hades all agreed. Demeter then brought spring to the world, turning it green and fruitful, so that everyone could celebrate her daughter's return. Ever since, for eight months of the year, the world has stayed green and bountiful while Persephone walks upon it. But when the time comes for her to return to the land of death, the world dies, too. It turns bleak and cold, only to be reborn each spring at her return.

HESTIA

Hestia was modest and shy. She never forced her presence on anyone, god or mortal. Because of that, there are no stories told about her; but in every Greek city there was a public hearth sacred to her, as the goddess of the hearth. Whenever a new city was begun, the people would carry coals from their old home on their journey. When they reached their new home, they kindled the fire on the new city's hearth and asked Hestia's blessing. It was believed that the safety of the city depended on protecting her sacred fire, so it never went out. She was the symbol of the home, and every house in ancient Greece held a shrine to her.

ATHENA

Athena's favorite bird was the owl, and she usually had a pet owl sitting on her shoulder: this is why even today we call owls wise. Athena taught Hephaestus how to use his tools, and taught mortals also. She showed them how to weave, how to make pots, and how to do other useful crafts.

The story of Athena's birth is a strange one. Her mother was Metis, Zeus' first wife, whom he had swallowed while Metis was pregnant. When it was time for Metis' child to be born, Zeus' head began to ache. He roared and howled in pain. Then all at once gray-eyed Athena emerged from his head, magically full

grown, wearing armor and carrying a shield. (She was also a goddess of battle, and when she fought, she always won. She even
bested Ares, the god of war.)

There once was a beautiful city in Greece that both Athena and
Poseidon loved and wanted for their own. Zeus declared that its
people should worship whichever of them gave it the best present.
Poseidon struck a rock with his trident and a spring gushed forth.
But it was salty seawater, and the people could not drink it.
Athena's gift was the olive tree. The olives and their oil were a
very useful gift, and the people declared her the winner. After that
the city was called Athens. In Athena's honor the people of
Athens worshiped wisdom over all other things.

Athena was usually very even-tempered. Once, though, she overheard a young woman named Arachne speaking. "I am the best
weaver in all the world," Arachne said. "In fact, I am a better
weaver than Athena herself!"

Athena frowned, because she took great pride in her weav-
ing—she had invented the craft, after all. And she disliked
bragging. Not only was it rude, it was disrespectful.

Athena disguised herself as an old woman and went to
Arachne. Politely she warned Arachne that boasting would get her
in trouble. Arachne laughed in her face.

All at once Athena appeared in her true form. "I challenge
you to a contest," she said. "We shall both weave a tapestry. We'll
see who is the best weaver."

Arachne's friends were awed and excited. They watched as
Athena wove a wonderful cloth showing the gods and goddesses
in all their splendor. Arachne wove as well, and her tapestry
seemed to be just as beautifully made. But she wove scenes of the

gods that showed them acting like fools. That added insult to injury, as far as Athena was concerned.

When Arachne's friends rashly said that they liked Arachne's tapestry the best, Athena lost her temper. She went to the weaver's loom and tore the tapestry in two. Then she touched Arachne's head and made her wise enough to see how rude her behavior had been. Suddenly Arachne was ashamed—and frightened. Her vanity had offended a goddess.

But it was too late to apologize. Athena turned her into a spider. "Weave your pictures in dark corners, from now on," Athena said. "And let everyone who sees a spider remember to be wise, not vain."

ARES

No act of cruelty ever gave Ares a bad night's sleep, for he was a bully who liked nothing better than to stir up trouble among the mortals. Then he would leap into his chariot and join the fight himself, cutting down people right and left. He didn't care who won or lost, as long as there was blood and suffering. His constant companion was Eris, the goddess of envy, who also liked to cause trouble. She had a beautiful golden apple that the gods called the Apple of Discord, because she used it to ruin friendships and set enemies to fighting. Ares' other vicious hangers-on included Panic, Pain, Famine, and Oblivion.

Like most bullies, Ares was not only cruel but also cowardly. Whenever he was wounded in battle, he would run back to Olympus, where his mother Hera would patiently bind up his scratches while he whined and screamed. The other gods held their ears, and Zeus swore that Ares was the worst of his children.

HEPHAESTUS

Hephaestus was born small and sickly, and Zeus disowned him, saying, "This weakling is no son of mine!" Zeus flung Hephaestus down from Mount Olympus. Hephaestus fell for seven days, until he struck the earth on the island of Lemnos. Thetis, a kind and gentle sea goddess, found the poor bruised baby there on the shore. She took care of him and nursed him back to health. But he had broken a leg so badly in the fall that he was lame forever after. He wore a leg brace made of gold.

Hephaestus was determined to show his father that he was not a weakling. The goddess Athena, his half-sister, felt their father had been very cruel. She helped Hephaestus grow into a strong and skillful man: she taught him to work metal, which gave him strong muscles and deft hands. Hephaestus built himself a forge on Lemnos, where he made wonderful things, including three-legged golden tables, which could run wherever he sent them, and golden maidens who helped him with his work. The Cyclopes, one-eyed giants who were skillful smiths, also worked for him.

At last Zeus admitted his mistake and invited Hephaestus back to Olympus to stay.

APHRODITE

No one knew who Aphrodite's parents were. She rose one day out of the foam of the sea, as beautiful as sunlight on the water. The wind, seeing the lovely woman adrift in a scallop shell, carried her to the island of Cyprus.

When the gods looked down and saw her, they knew she must be a goddess herself, for wherever she stepped, flowers sprang up, and the air smelled as sweet as spring. They sent her shining robes to wear and brought her up to Olympus. All the gods present fell madly in love with her at first sight. To avoid arguments and discord, Zeus gave her in marriage to his son Hephaestus. He wanted to show his rejected son how sorry he was for treating him badly. Besides, he could tell that Aphrodite was rather impulsive and liked to flirt. (Since he was sometimes the same way, he knew the signs.) He felt that a good, solid fellow like Hephaestus would make the best husband for her. Aphrodite agreed to marry Hephaestus, since she wanted to continue her new, splendid life among the gods.

Hephaestus felt that he was the luckiest god alive to have such a beautiful wife. He showered her with gifts, hoping to make her happy. One of the gifts of jewelry was a golden girdle—a magic belt that made anyone who wore it irresistible. (Not that Aphrodite really needed such a thing.)

Unfortunately Aphrodite did not appreciate her plainspoken, rather bashful husband's gifts or his talent. She saw only a sweaty, dull fellow who spent too much time working. She hated it when he got soot on her silken robes. She loved passion and glamour and physical beauty. She would much rather have been married to Hephaestus' handsome brother Ares, the god of war.

All Aphrodite could see was that Ares was extremely good-looking. She had always had trouble understanding that beauty was only skin deep, since her own beauty had brought her so many good things. She never saw how Ares behaved on the battle-field—she only heard him bragging about his deeds and thought him bold and exciting. She was certain that no one else really understood him.

Not surprisingly, Ares felt the same way about Aphrodite that she felt about him, especially when she wore her golden girdle. Hephaestus saw them staring at each other across the hall whenever the council met. When he complained to the other gods, though, they only said, "Well, then, why did you make that girdle for her?" He wished he knew.

ARTEMIS

Artemis was as fair as the moon, with night-black hair. She was also fiercely independent, even as a little girl. One day her father, Zeus, sat her on his knee and asked what gift she would like from him. She asked him to promise that she would never have to marry. She wanted to be free to live her own life, enjoying the beautiful hills and forests, with only her friends, the young nymphs of wood and river, as her companions. Zeus was surprised by this request; but then, his other daughter, Athena, was also a strong, independent-minded goddess. *They must take after me,* he decided. He told Artemis that she could have her wish.

Artemis was very happy. She became the Chief Huntsman of the gods, and drove to the chase in a magnificent chariot drawn by four stags with golden antlers. Her silver bow and arrows were made for her by Hephaestus. The bow was shaped like the crescent moon, for Artemis was also the moon goddess. Her arrows were magic and caused no pain, for Artemis did not like to bring needless suffering to any creature she hunted. She also took special care of young animals and was the protector of children.

Artemis was not cruel by nature, but she guarded her independence and privacy fiercely. Perhaps because of her mother's suffering, she had little tolerance for any man who threatened her freedom.

Once the mortal prince Actaeon was out hunting by night with his hounds. Wandering away from his friends, he chanced upon the moonlit lake where Artemis and the nymphs were bathing. He stopped in awe at the sight of the goddess standing moon-white in the dark, glittering water. He should have known better. Instead of running for his life, he kept watching, hypnotized by Artemis' beauty.

The goddess looked up and saw a stranger watching her. She thought he meant to hurt her. At the very least, he would go back to his friends and brag that he had seen a goddess bathing, and they would all mock her.

Outraged, she flung a handful of water at Actaeon. As the silvery droplets struck him, he turned into a stag. Terrified, he turned and ran. But it was too late. His own hounds set upon him and killed him. His friends never knew what had become of him. Only Artemis knew, and she felt no remorse at his terrible fate.

The only man Artemis ever showed much fondness for was the handsome young giant Orion, a son of Poseidon. Orion was a great hunter himself, but he was a modest youth and always mentioned Artemis as his ideal when he spoke of hunting.

Once Orion went to Crete, Artemis' favorite island. As she saw his tall, handsome profile against the night sky, she was taken by his beauty and manly grace. She invited him to go hunting with her. They had a wonderful time ranging through the hills and glens together.

Artemis might have decided to give up her solitary life and

The goddess looked up and saw a stranger watching her.

marry the dashing huntsman who admired her so. But her brother, Apollo, prevented that. He and Artemis had always been very close, as twins often are. Apollo could not stand the thought of Orion stealing his sister away. He sent a giant scorpion to sting Orion on the heel. Its poison was strong enough to kill even the mighty hunter.

When Orion died, Artemis was grief-stricken. She asked Zeus to put Orion up in the heavens as a constellation, so that when she hunted at night she could see him there among the stars. Zeus granted her request. But every night as Orion the Hunter rises from below the horizon to stride across the sky, he is followed by the starry form of Scorpio, the giant scorpion.

Artemis was angry with Apollo for a long time, but eventually she forgave him. They had always been inseparable.

APOLLO

Apollo carried a bow and arrows, too, and it was Artemis who taught him how to shoot. Apollo's arrows were not the silent, silver ones that brought death without pain. They were hard and bright, and brought a burning, painful death to people who acted unjustly.

Apollo rarely used his arrows; most of the time he was a good and noble god. He was as beautiful and bright as sunlight. In fact, he was often called Phoebus, which means *bright* or *shining*. Apollo was the god of light, and the only god besides Helios, the sun god, who was allowed to drive Helios' sun chariot across the skies. He was also the god of unmarried men—for like his sister,

Artemis, he never formally married (although he had a number of mortal wives and sweethearts).

Apollo's favorite spot on earth was Delphi, where he had an oracle. An oracle was a special place where mortals who had questions or requests for a god could go to get answers. Delphi, on the slopes of Mount Parnassus, was the most sacred oracle of all.

At the Delphic Oracle, a priestess called a sibyl sat on a three-legged stool above a crack in the earth. Sulfurous fumes rose from the depths far below her. As she inhaled them, she slipped into a trance and spoke the wisdom of the gods.

Once, the Delphic oracle had belonged to Mother Earth. It was surrounded by the coils of a vast, ancient dragon as dark as night. He was called Python, and he had been told by Mother Earth to defend the oracle. Zeus and Mother Earth were not on the best of terms, however, so when Apollo was full grown, Zeus sent him to claim the oracle for himself.

Python had been warned by the oracle that someday Leto's son would come to kill him. Now at last he saw Apollo coming down out of the sky in his radiant chariot. Python knew that he was doomed. Still he put up a ferocious fight: he breathed out huge waves of fire and sent his venom down in rivers along the slopes of Parnassus. His dark, scaly body writhed and thrashed as he tried to crush Apollo in its coils. Not until Apollo had fired a thousand burning arrows into Python's flesh did the dreadful monster die.

The lands around the oracle had been filled with darkness and fear while the dragon lay coiled at their heart. Now that Python was gone, Apollo sang and played his golden lyre, and the lands were filled with light and music.

Most nymphs and mortal maidens found Apollo hard to resist, for he was not only brave but heartbreakingly handsome. He was thoughtful and romantic when he courted them, singing love songs and treating them with gallantry.

Apollo's first love was the only one who ever spurned him. Eros, the mischievous little son of Aphrodite, made the young Apollo fall in love with a beautiful nymph named Daphne. Eros also carried a bow and arrows—and anyone struck by his arrow fell helplessly in love with the first person he or she saw. Apollo had foolishly teased little Eros about his miniature weapons, and Eros decided to teach Apollo a lesson.

Struck in the heart by Eros' shaft, Apollo saw Daphne and chased her through the forest. He pleaded with her to come and be his love. But Daphne, the daughter of a river god, was a follower of Artemis. She loved her freedom as much as Apollo's sister did. Daphne knew that marriage to a god not only meant the end of her freedom but often brought terrible troubles with it. She ran swiftly, but so did Apollo.

Just as he was about to catch her, she called out to her father to help her. Suddenly her feet became rooted to the ground. Her clothing turned to smooth brown bark. Her uplifted hands turned into branches, sprouting leaves, and she became a laurel tree.

Apollo was filled with amazement and sorrow. He touched the new tree's branches and felt them tremble. He hugged its trunk. "Since you will not be my wife," he said, "you will become my sacred tree. I will wear your leaves as my crown and never forget you. All the winners at my games and great heroes in the years to come will be crowned with laurel leaves. And, like me, you will have eternal youth. Your leaves will never turn brown or fall, but

Her uplifted hands turned into branches, sprouting leaves, and she became a laurel tree.

will always stay green." The nymph, hiding safely within her tree, bowed her head and nodded gratefully. Apollo left her side wearing a crown of laurel leaves.

HERMES

Hermes' mother was Maia, a Titan's daughter. She lived in a cave hidden so deep inside Mother Earth that Hera never knew Maia had married Zeus. As a result, Maia was able to give birth to Hermes without any trouble from Hera.

Hermes grew with amazing speed, like most young gods. His mother went to sleep cuddling her new baby against her side, and by the time she woke up again, he had already begun to cause mischief.

After a short nap, Hermes climbed out of their bed, toddled outside the cave, and wandered down the road. He discovered a fine herd of cattle grazing in a nearby field. He decided to take them back to his mother. He did not know that the cattle he was planning to steal belonged to Apollo. He only knew that he wanted to impress his father and the other gods on Olympus with his cleverness. He wanted them to notice him so that he could take his rightful place among them.

Hermes stole fifty of the finest cows in the herd. He didn't want their owner to follow their tracks to his cave, because he knew that whoever owned them would be very angry with him. So he made shoes of oak bark and tied them onto the cows' hooves to disguise their tracks. He attached brooms to their tails to sweep away more of their trail. Then, still in the middle of the night, he drove them home backward.

Apollo searched high and low for his cattle, but Hermes' trick had erased all trace of them. At last Apollo offered a reward to anyone who could tell him where they had gone.

The old forest god Silenus, who was half man and half goat, and his followers, the goat-footed satyrs, wanted the reward. They searched everywhere, until at last they heard beautiful music coming from the mouth of a cave. A nymph told them an amazing child had been born there. The child had fashioned a wonderful musical instrument, called a lyre, from tortoiseshell and cow gut. The suspicious satyrs noticed two cowhides hanging outside the cave and called Apollo.

Apollo went into the cave. Hermes was lying innocently in his cradle, but Apollo wasn't fooled. He took Hermes under his arm and carried him off to Olympus. He accused the little boy of theft in front of all the other gods. Zeus refused to believe that Hermes (whom he knew was his son) was guilty. But finally Hermes admitted he had stolen the cattle. "I slaughtered only two and cut them up into twelve equal parts, as an offering to the twelve gods of Olympus," he said.

"Twelve gods?" Apollo asked. He knew of only eleven. "Who is the twelfth?"

"I am," Hermes said, and bowed modestly. "I ate no more than my share."

"Well, you still did a bad thing," Apollo said irritably. "How will you pay me back for my cattle?"

Hermes took Apollo to his mother's cave and showed him the tortoiseshell lyre. Hermes played the lyre and sang a song praising Apollo's goodness and generosity. Apollo was so surprised and pleased that he gave Hermes all the stolen cattle in return for the lyre.

The two gods returned to Olympus. Zeus warned Hermes never to tell lies or steal anything again, although he was secretly amused by his son's antics.

Hermes asked to become the gods' herald, carrying their messages to earth. "I will never lie again," he said, then added, "although I might not tell the whole truth."

"You won't be expected to," Zeus answered. He gave Hermes a herald's staff with white ribbons, a winged golden hat to protect him from sun and rain, a magic cape, and winged golden sandals to carry him like the wind.

Hades also made Hermes his herald. Hermes went to all who were dying. He called them gently and kindly to follow him down to the underworld.

DIONYSUS

Dionysus was the only one of the gods whose mother was a mortal. But, as was true for many of the gods, his father was Zeus. Every night while Hera lay sleeping, Zeus had flown down from Olympus to be with Dionysus' mother, a Theban princess named Semele.

One night Hera woke and followed Zeus. She discovered the latest of the young women he was always marrying. As usual, Hera felt jealous. Before Dionysus was born, Hera visited Semele, disguised as her old nursemaid. Hera chatted with Semele and then asked innocently about Semele's husband. Semele said proudly that her husband was Zeus himself.

Hera pretended to be surprised. "How do you know it's

true?" she asked. "Has he given you any proof? Anyone can claim he is a god. Ask him to show you how he really looks, in all his splendor, so that you can be certain." She left, and Semele sat alone with her doubts all day.

When Zeus returned, Semele asked him for a favor. Zeus never suspected what it would be. He was very much in love with her, so he agreed. He swore by the River Styx—an oath that even the gods could not break—that he would grant her any wish.

He was horrified when he heard her request, for any mortal who saw a god's true appearance would die. He begged her to change her request. But that made her even more suspicious, and she refused. Zeus could not break his oath. He cast off his disguise of a handsome, richly dressed man, and stood before her in the blinding brilliance of his true godly splendor. The room shook with thunder, and lightning cracked its walls.

The terrified princess burst into flames and burned to ash. Zeus could do nothing to save her. But he managed to rescue her unborn child, who was immortal, just as he was.

Zeus gave the infant to Hermes. Hermes took Dionysus to be raised by nymphs who lived in a hidden valley. There he had a happy childhood, with leopard and tiger cubs for playmates. When he grew older, he discovered how to make wine from the grapes that grew everywhere around him in the valley.

When he had grown to manhood, Dionysus wandered the earth, teaching mortals how to make wine. Everywhere they greeted him as a new god and made him welcome. Zeus looked down from Olympus and smiled.

Once during his travels Dionysus met pirates who were sailing along the coast. When they saw the splendid youth, with his long dark curls and his cloak of royal purple, they thought that he must be a prince. They kidnapped him and decided to hold him for ransom. Dionysus tried to warn them that he was a god and that his riches were not of this earth. They only laughed.

On board their ship the pirates tied him up, but to their astonishment the ropes fell away from him. Acetes, the ship's helmsman, realized that Dionysus was telling them the truth, and begged the others to set Dionysus free. The captain called Acetes a fool and ordered him to sail on.

But suddenly the ship could not move. Red wine began to flow over the deck. A grapevine grew up the mast, and ivy twined around the oars. The sailors ordered the helmsman to head back to shore. But it was too late. The air filled with the roaring of invisible beasts. Tigers and leopards crouched at Dionysus' feet, and he held a spear twined with ivy.

The terrified sailors began to leap overboard. Acetes, the helmsman, pleaded with Dionysus not to let his friends drown. Dionysus decided to show them mercy: rather than allowing them to die, he changed them into dolphins. Ever since, dolphins have been the most human creatures in the sea.

Dionysus spread much happiness through the world, and at last Zeus decided that it was time for him to take his place on Olympus. Hera protested, saying, "His mother is only a mortal!" Zeus roared and thundered and insisted until Hera finally gave in.

When Dionysus arrived on Olympus, his first request to his father was to see Semele, the mother he had never known. Zeus said, "Not only can you see her, but you may bring her here to live with us. Tell Hades he must allow her to leave the underworld and come back with you. She may be only a mortal, but she is the mother of a god and deserves to live among the gods on Olympus."

Dionysus happily did so. When he returned he found his golden throne waiting for him. There was a grand celebration in the hall.

The other gods of Olympus loved to be worshiped in splendid temples, with the proper rituals and offerings. Dionysus, however, had no temples. His followers, who were mostly women, worshiped Dionysus in the wild. They left the crowded cities to sleep in the sweet meadows or on beds of pine boughs beneath the open sky. There Dionysus gave them all they needed—berries and fruits to eat, and the milk of wild goats to drink. They bathed in the clear waters of streams and lakes. They were filled with the peace and beauty of the natural world. Their lives far from civilization were free and joyful.

Yet there was a dark side to Dionysus and his worship. When mortals failed to show him proper respect, the ferocity of Dionysus' anger blazed, and he drove them mad. His followers, the maenads, would sometimes drink wine until they lost their senses. Then they would run through the forests in a mindless frenzy, waving pinecone-tipped wands. Anything they came upon—animal or human—they would tear to pieces.

The worship of Dionysus was based on two ideas that were as far apart as the poles of the earth—joyous freedom and terrible violence. His worship was like the nature of wine itself, which is both bad and good. Wine can bring high spirits; it can also bring pain and ugliness to those who drink too much of it.

Despite his dark side, Dionysus became not only the god of wine but also the god of inspiration. Writers and other artists worshiped him. Each spring when the grapevines began to show new leaves, a festival was held in Dionysus' honor. His festival was celebrated not in a temple, but in the open air, with plays and poetry. Dionysus himself often attended the festivals in disguise, sitting unrecognized among his followers to watch the plays, some of which are still performed today.

MINOR GODS
AND GODDESSES

Though they did not have special seats in the great hall and rarely had a voice in important decisions, many other gods and goddesses lived on Olympus. The most important of these were the three Fates—Clotho, Lachesis, and Atropos. These three sisters spun the destinies of all creatures. They knew the past and the future, and the day on which each and every creature would die. Zeus himself could not keep the Fates from snipping the thread of a life line that had run out.

There were also many lesser gods and goddesses who lived on the earth and never left it for the halls of Olympus. They watched over the streams and forests, over the creatures of land and sea, and they punished any mortal who took the bounty of nature without showing the proper gratitude and respect. There were also many fairylike nymphs and dryads living peacefully in the forests, springs, and streams.

Sharing the unspoiled land with them were the satyrs— followers of the nature god Pan—who were half human and half goat. Pan was both shy and wild, like a forest creature. He often slept in caves. If someone passing by happened to wake him, he would give a loud bellow. His sudden shouts in the quiet forest gave travelers quite a start—a feeling we still call *panic*, after Pan.

There were also the centaurs, half human and half horse. Because they were part animal, the centaurs and satyrs were often wild and badly behaved. Mortals sometimes befriended them, but were usually sorry they had. When invited to weddings and feasts, centaurs and satyrs always drank too much and invariably caused a scene.

THE FIRST
HUMAN BEINGS

When Zeus decided that the earth needed living creatures to pay the gods proper respect, he asked
Prometheus, the wisest of the Titans, to create
them. Zeus was certain that Prometheus would do the best job.

Prometheus was eager to take on the task. Unfortunately he
did one unwise thing—he asked his brother Epimetheus to join
him. Prometheus' name means *forethought*. His brother
Epimetheus' name means *afterthought*. Epimetheus was as thought-
less as Prometheus was wise, but still Prometheus loved him.

Together they modeled animals and people out of clay. Zeus
had given them special gifts to bestow on each of the creatures
into which they breathed life.

Prometheus worked on creating human beings, fashioning
them in the image of the gods. He gave Epimetheus the lesser
task of creating animals, thinking that would be a safe enough
job. Prometheus worked slowly and carefully, while Epimetheus
created his designs with lightning speed. Before Prometheus was
finished, Epimetheus had heedlessly given all the best gifts of the
gods to the animals: the animals could run faster, and see and
smell and hear better, than humans. Most of them were stronger,
too. They had fur coats to keep them warm, while people shiv-
ered from the cold at night.

Prometheus was angry with his brother, but he could not
change what had already been done. He loved his own creations,

the human beings, and hated to see them shivering and starving. He asked Zeus if he could give humans the gift of fire, to warm and help protect them.

Zeus refused. He said that fire belonged only to the gods. Prometheus took a deep breath and made a silent decision. He would steal fire and give it to his mortal children. He was afraid that Zeus would punish him for it, but he felt that he must act for the greater good. He went secretly to Athena, who, he knew, was the fairest and most reasonable of the gods. She agreed to help him and told him how he could steal an ember from the sacred hearth.

Prometheus carried the ember down to earth, and showed the people he had created how to keep their fires burning. He warned them that they must never let the fires go out. The people were overjoyed. The fire warmed them and kept them safe at night, for wild animals fled from the sight of it. Soon the humans even learned to cook their food over it.

As they watched the smoke rise up to heaven, their hearts filled with gratitude. They sang songs of praise, giving thanks to the gods for sending them such a gift. They made offerings of meat placed in the fire. The gods did not eat meat—they preferred nectar and ambrosia—but they enjoyed the pleasant smell of food cooking that the smoke carried up to them.

Zeus was, of course, very angry to learn what Prometheus had done. But the scent of burnt offerings and the voices of humankind rising up on the smoke with songs of praise and thanks pleased him greatly. His anger eased. He told Prometheus gruffly that he would let the humans keep fire as long as they remembered to make plentiful offerings to the gods.

Prometheus gave a sigh of relief. Still, he worried about his mortal creations. He felt it was unfair that the gods demanded as

Prometheus carried the ember down to earth...

offerings the best of the food humans worked so hard for. So Prometheus instructed them to butcher a cow and divide the carcass into two piles. In one pile they were to put all the best edible meat and cover it with bones. In the other pile they were to put the inedible hooves, hides, and scraps, and cover them with a thick layer of rich fat.

He then invited the gods to choose which pile they preferred. Of course the gods chose the pile covered with rich fat. They were outraged to discover what lay beneath it. Zeus realized that Prometheus had tricked him again. "This is unforgivable!" he said. "First you stole fire. Then you made fools of us! You will be punished!"

Prometheus was chained to an isolated rock high in the Caucasus Mountains. Every day a vulture flew down and tore out his liver. Because Prometheus was immortal, every night his liver grew back, only to be torn out again the next day. Prometheus suffered great agony, but he never regretted what he had done for humanity. He remained proud of his defiant acts. All human beings honored him for his courage and his refusal to bow to an unjust oppressor, even if the oppressor was Zeus himself.

PANDORA'S JAR

Zeus decided to win back the favor both of the mortals and of Epimetheus, Prometheus' brother. He had Hephaestus create a beautiful woman named Pandora. She was to be Epimetheus' wife, and her marriage gifts were to bring blessings from the gods to humanity. Each god and goddess gave Pandora a precious gift—joy, peace, trust, kindness, generosity, health. All of these were contained in a jeweled jar, which Zeus warned Pandora never to open.

Epimetheus was delighted to have such a lovely wife, and mortals were also delighted to have her among them, bringing them such wonderful gifts. Pandora and Epimetheus got along very well.

But Pandora proved to be as impulsive as her husband. She wondered constantly what joy and peace actually looked like. One day her curiosity overcame her, and she opened the lid of the beautiful jar.

The gods' blessed gifts flew out around her like birds and escaped into the air. Pandora slammed the lid down, trapping only the very last of the gifts—hope. Ever since, all human joy and good fortune have been fleeting; but hope always remains, to help people bear life's burdens.

...and she opened the lid of the beautiful jar.

THE GREAT FLOOD

Prometheus had a son named Deucalion. Deucalion loved his father very much, and he came to visit the place where Prometheus was held captive as often as he could. Deucalion could not set his father free, but he brought him food and drove away the vulture that came to torture him.

One day Prometheus, who had visions of the future, told his son that a great flood was coming. Humans, who had lived in peace and plenty at first, had begun to grow greedy and cruel. People were forging weapons of war instead of tools for building and farming. They were cutting down the forests and poisoning the waters of Mother Earth. They were not honoring the gods. Zeus had become so angry with them that he had decided to get rid of them all.

Deucalion was terrified when he heard this. But Prometheus said, "Don't be afraid. You can save yourself and your wife. Build a ship and fill it with everything you'll need. Be ready."

Deucalion nodded. He ran home and told his beloved wife, Pyrrha. Together they built their boat. Just as they finished loading it, the first drops of rain began to fall. They hurried on board.

It rained for nine days and nine nights, until the whole world was flooded and only the highest mountain peaks still showed. Only Deucalion and Pyrrha survived.

On the tenth day the rain stopped. The boat drifted on, until at last the waters began to recede and land slowly reappeared. The ship ran aground on the slope of a mountain, near a ruined temple. Hand in hand Deucalion and Pyrrha left the ark and walked through the mud to the seaweed-hung temple. They rekindled its sacred fire with an ember they had carried on their ship. Then they gave thanks to the gods for sparing them. And because they were all alone, they prayed to the gods for help.

Realizing that they were good and deserving, Zeus took pity on them. "Pick up the bones of your mother," he told them, "and throw them over your shoulder."

Pyrrha turned pale as she heard the god's voice speaking to them from out of the air. "It is a sacrilege to disturb the bones of our ancestors!" she protested.

Deucalion shook his head. "This is a test of our wisdom," he told her. "The god doesn't mean the bones of our real mothers. He means Mother Earth." Deucalion picked up a handful of stones and told his wife to do the same. They began to pitch rocks over their shoulders. And where each of Deucalion's stones fell, men sprang up behind him. Women sprang up where Pyrrha's stones fell. These new people, sprung from stone, were a hardy race, stronger than those who had come before.

Deucalion and Pyrrha went on to live long, contented lives. They were revered as the founders of a new race, just as Prometheus once had been.

PERSEUS
AND MEDUSA

King Acrisius of Argos had a beautiful daughter named Danaë, but he was not happy. He wanted a son to be king after him. He went to the oracle at Delphi to ask if he would ever have another child.

The oracle told him he would never have a son. And worse, his daughter would have a son who would one day kill him. The only way Acrisius could prevent this was to kill his daughter immediately.

Acrisius was a cold, ruthless man, and now he was frightened as well. But he did not dare to kill his daughter. People who killed members of their own family were punished harshly by the gods. Hades would send the Furies—three fearsome, black-clad women carrying whips—to follow him wherever he fled, tormenting him.

So instead of killing his daughter, Acrisius imprisoned her. He put her in a bronze house sunk deep into the ground. There were only narrow window slits just below its roof to let in light and air. All Danaë could see were the stars at night and in the daytime the clouds drifting by.

Zeus, looking down from Olympus, saw the unhappy maiden and fell in love with her. He changed himself into a shower of gold and entered her prison window. A wonderful voice spoke from inside the golden cloud, telling Danaë that she was not forgotten. Zeus himself loved her and would watch over her.

After a while a child was born to Danaë and Zeus. The baby

He changed himself into a shower of gold...

was a boy, and Danaë named him Perseus. She was delighted to have her baby with her, to fill her lonely days.

But it was hard to keep anything hidden from her father, and soon Perseus was discovered. Acrisius was sure this was the child who would kill him. Still he did not dare to kill his daughter or her son.

Instead he had a large chest built and locked Danaë and her baby inside it. Then he set them adrift on the sea. "Now if they die it will be Poseidon's fault, not mine," he muttered.

Danaë and her baby drifted in the chest all that day. That night a storm swept over the sea. Danaë heard the wind moaning and felt the waves batter her strange little ark. She held her son close, singing him songs and rocking him in her arms. Holding him through the night, she found comfort in his sweet sleeping face and shining curls. She said a prayer to Zeus, asking for his help.

Just as dawn broke, she felt a great wave lift them up and drop them onto solid ground. They had washed ashore on an island. They were safe—though still trapped in the box.

But not for long. Dictys, a fisherman, saw the chest and was amazed to hear voices coming from inside it. He broke the lock and helped the weary mother and her son out. He took them to his wife, who was as kind as he was. She gave them dry clothes and fed them. The couple had no children of their own, and so they treated Danaë and Perseus like their own daughter and grandson.

Danaë and Perseus lived in the fishing village very happily. Danaë did not miss her old life as a princess, for the people, though poor, were far kinder than her own family. She was glad to have Perseus grow up learning only the ways of a simple fisherman. She thought they would be safe always.

But ahead lay dangers she never suspected. Dictys' brother, Polydectes, was the king of the small island on which they lived. The two brothers rarely saw each other. Like Danaë, Dictys preferred fisherfolk to the company of his royal relatives. So it was many years before Polydectes learned that his brother had adopted a family. By that time Perseus was a young man. Polydectes stopped in to see his brother while traveling around the island. He fell in love with Danaë when he met her, for she was still very beautiful. He wanted to marry her.

He did not want Perseus, however. *Why,* he thought, *should a stranger's son inherit my kingdom?* He would have his own children with Danaë and get rid of Perseus. But Polydectes kept his thoughts to himself. He brought Danaë and Perseus to his palace and treated them both very well.

Then Polydectes told Perseus that his fondest wish was to have the head of Medusa brought to him. Medusa was one of the three Gorgons—scaly, winged monsters with women's faces and snakes for hair. Any mortal who looked into their eyes was doomed—turned to stone by their terrible gaze.

After telling Perseus of his wish, Polydectes announced that he and Danaë would be married. All his nobles vied for the honor of giving them the most impressive wedding gift. Perseus, who had always been poor, had nothing to give. He felt ashamed, as Polydectes had known he would. Perseus wanted to make his new stepfather proud of him. He stood up and announced that he would bring Polydectes the best gift of all—Medusa's head. Polydectes was pleased. He was sure Perseus would die trying to kill Medusa.

That night, before his mother could learn of his plan and try to stop him, Perseus took his fishing boat and sailed away. He went first to Delphi and asked the oracle how he could find Medusa's lair. He was told to travel to the land of Dodona, where the oak trees spoke and people ate acorns instead of grain. There the oaks whispered to Perseus that he was under the protection of the gods. They did not, however, tell him where to find Medusa.

As Perseus went on his way, growing weary and discouraged, another young man joined him on the road. Perseus recognized the youth's winged sandals and helmet: the god Hermes, Zeus' messenger, was walking beside him.

"Zeus sent me to help you," Hermes told Perseus. "You need magic weapons or you will never defeat Medusa." Hermes gave Perseus two magic objects: a sword that could pierce Medusa's scales and Hades' cap of invisibility. "I will also loan you my winged shoes," he added.

"That isn't all," said another voice. Perseus turned to find his half-sister, gray-eyed Athena, standing behind him. Like Hermes, she was eager to help Perseus defeat Medusa. "Take my silver bag," she said. "It stretches to hold anything you put inside it. And here is my shield. You must use it as a mirror when you find Medusa. Look at her reflection when you fight. Never look directly at her, or you will turn to stone."

"How will I find her?" Perseus asked. "No one seems to know where she lives."

"The only ones who know that are the Graiae—the three Gray Sisters," Hermes said. "I'll lead you to them."

"Once there, you must steal their eye," Athena told him. "That is the only way you can force them to tell you where Medusa is."

Hermes took Perseus to the strange land where the Gray Sisters lived. The sun never rose or set there. Everything was forever dim and gray, frozen in eternal twilight.

The Graiae sat among the gray stones, cackling and muttering to one another. Perseus had never seen anything so strange. At first, the Gray Sisters seemed to be giant birds, for they had the shape of swans. But there were human arms and hands beneath their wings.

Strangest of all, they had only one eye among them, and they took turns using it. Each sister plucked the eye out of her forehead and passed it to the next one for a time.

Perseus, who now understood Athena's instructions, waited behind a rock until one of the sisters removed the eye and held it in her hand. He leaped out before she could pass it on and grabbed it from her.

Now the Graiae could not see at all. Thinking they had dropped the eye, they scrabbled about in the dim half-light searching for it.

"I have your eye!" Perseus called. "Tell me where the Gorgons are, and I'll give it back."

The Sisters immediately told him the way. They would have done anything to get their eye back.

Perseus handed the eye to a Gray Sister. Then he waved farewell to Hermes and leaped into the air. With the help of Hermes' winged sandals he flew swiftly to the midnight land of the Gorgons.

When Perseus arrived, the Gorgons were sleeping, stretched out before the entrance of their cave with their wings furled and their hideous faces hidden. All around them stone statues littered the bare, rocky ground. Perseus stared in horror: those statues had once been flesh-and-blood warriors. They had all been turned to stone by the Gorgons' gaze.

"Only Medusa is mortal," Athena whispered to Perseus. She showed him which of the dreadful sisters Medusa was.

Perseus hovered over Medusa and shouted loudly to wake her, for he could not strike off her head until she raised it. But once she woke he could look at her only in his shield, using it for a mirror, as Athena had told him to do.

Medusa raised her head with a snarl. So did her sisters. Perseus did not dare to look into their eyes, afraid he would turn to stone like all the rest. Every move he made felt wrong; everything he did was backward in the mirror. When Perseus saw the reflection of Medusa's hideous face, writhing with snakes, he shuddered. And yet the urge to turn toward her real face and look into her eyes was so strong he could barely resist it.

Instead he raised Hermes' shining sword high and brought it down with all his strength. Medusa's head fell to the ground. From her headless neck there rose a sudden flurry of blinding white wings: a magic horse, born of her blood, soared into the sky glowing like the moon. Perseus was so surprised that he almost forgot to keep his eyes on the mirror. He saw the reflection of the other Gorgons—who could not be killed—flash across his shield as they lunged at him.

Perseus grabbed Medusa's head by a handful of squirming snakes. He stuffed the head into Athena's silver bag, where the face would be safely hidden. (Even dead, Medusa still had the power to turn people to stone.) Then he leaped into the air again,

...he raised Hermes' shining sword high and brought it down with all his strength.

barely escaping the grasping hands of Medusa's sisters, and flew away.

As Perseus traveled back to Polydectes' island, he flew over the land of Ethiopia. Looking down, he saw a beautiful young woman chained to a rocky ledge above the sea. On a cliff, a crowd of people wept and lamented. Wondering how she had come to be in such a terrible situation, Perseus flew down to her side.

"Who are you?" he asked. "What has happened to you?"

Frightened by the stranger who had appeared so suddenly beside her, the woman at first would not speak to him.

"Why are you here?" Perseus asked again. "Can I help you?"

"My name is Andromeda," she said at last. "My father is the king of Ethiopia. My mother, Queen Cassiopeia, insulted the sea god Nereus. She said she was more beautiful than all his fifty daughters." Nereus had sent floods and storms over their land as a punishment. He demanded that Andromeda be left as a sacrifice, to be eaten by a sea monster.

Just then the water began to boil and roll below them. The monstrous head of a gigantic sea beast rose from the waves. Its jaws were open, its hundred teeth gleamed, and its red throat was ready to swallow them both.

Perseus drew his sword and leaped into the air. He stabbed the thrashing, roaring monster again and again, until, mortally wounded, it sank beneath the surface once more.

Perseus broke Andromeda's chains with his sword and carried her through the air to the top of the cliff. There her astonished father and mother, and all her family, cheered and embraced them.

"Young man, you may have any reward I can bestow," said the king, "for saving the life of my daughter!"

"Then let me marry her and take her home with me," said Perseus. "I love her already."

"With our blessing!" cried the grateful queen. So Perseus and Andromeda were married with much celebration. After the wedding feast, Perseus carried her back to his island home.

When they arrived, he learned that his mother, Danaë, and old Dictys (whose wife had died long ago) were in hiding. Danaë had refused to marry Polydectes when she learned how he had tricked Perseus into going after Medusa. The king in turn became so enraged that Danaë and Dictys were forced to flee for their lives.

Perseus went directly to Polydectes' palace. There the ruthless king was giving a banquet for all his nobles. When Perseus appeared in the great hall carrying Athena's shining shield and the sword of Hermes, they looked up from their meal in amazement.

"Here is your wedding present!" cried Perseus. He pulled Medusa's head from its pouch and held it up for the king and all his nobles to see. As their eyes fell on Medusa's hideous face, they were instantly turned to stone. Forever after, they sat at the table gaping sightlessly toward the door.

Athena and Hermes appeared before Perseus as he left the palace. "Congratulations, son of Zeus," they said. He gave them back their weapons with many thanks. He also gave them Medusa's head; Athena bore it on her shield ever after.

When the islanders learned that cruel Polydectes was dead, they rejoiced. Danaë and Dictys came out of hiding, knowing they were safe at last. Danaë was happily reunited with her son, and she welcomed her new daughter-in-law. The people of the island made Dictys their new king.

Now Danaë longed to go back to her homeland. She thought that perhaps since her son had become a great hero, things would be different there and her father might welcome them home. So she, Perseus, and Andromeda sailed to Argos.

When they arrived, they learned that Acrisius was no longer king. The people had grown tired of his harsh rule and driven him away. Perseus and his family settled in Argos and lived peacefully for many years.

One day Perseus traveled north to Larissa to take part in the athletic games there. While he was competing in the discus throw, his discus flew off course. It struck and killed someone in the crowd. The victim was Acrisius, who had come to Larissa to visit the king. The oracle's prophecy had come true at last. Try as he would, Acrisius had not been able to escape his fate.

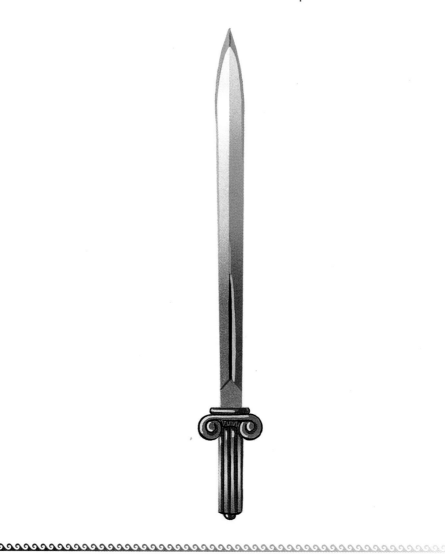

PHAËTHON

Phaëthon was a lonely, unhappy little boy. All the other boys he knew had fathers at home, but he had none. His mother had told him that his father was Helios, the sun god, whose daily duties kept him far away. But when Phaëthon told this to the other boys, they laughed at him.

At last Phaëthon grew old enough to journey to the sun god's palace, far in the east. He was determined to confront Helios, and learn whether the sun god was truly his father. When he arrived at the edge of the world, Helios' palace, all gold and jewels, shone with such fiery glory that Phaëthon had to shield his eyes. Barely able to see, he stumbled often as he climbed the steps and entered the great hall.

Helios sat on his throne crowned by rays of light. His own radiance was blinding—Phaëthon could not even look at him. The sun sees all things, though, and Helios saw the boy standing below him in the palace hall. Helios took off his crown so that the boy could look at him. When he did, Helios saw that Phaëthon's eyes were golden. All of Helios' children had golden eyes, and so he realized that this boy must be his son.

"My mother, whose name is Clymene, says you are my father," Phaëthon said. "But no one believes it. Is it true?"

"Yes, it is," Helios said. He was deeply touched that the boy had come all this way to see him, and pleased to see what a fine, handsome youth he was. Helios had loved Phaëthon's mother greatly, but only during an eclipse could he escape from his duties to visit the earth. "I will prove it to you. I will grant any wish you ask of me. I swear it by the River Styx." This, of course, was the one vow even gods could not break.

Phaëthon's golden eyes shone with excitement. "Oh, Father," he said, "let me drive your chariot across the sky for one day!"

Helios was stunned. He had never imagined that this would be his son's request. "My son," he said, "ask me anything else. I cannot refuse you, because I made an unbreakable promise. But what you ask for is terribly dangerous!" He explained how every morning when he set out, the path his chariot followed into the heights of the sky was so steep that even his horses, fresh from their rest, could scarcely climb up it. "And when I reach the heights, even I can hardly bear to look down, I am so far above the earth. When I begin the final downward arc, Poseidon himself cannot believe that I do not tumble from my chariot into the sea."

Helios warned his son further that his horses were incredibly strong. They would run away with another driver, especially one who was only a boy. "Please change your mind," he begged. "Let my fear for your safety prove that you really are my son, and that I love you."

But Phaëthon, who had watched his father's wondrous passage across the sky for so long, shook his head. It had been his fondest dream to drive that chariot one day. His father's warning fell on deaf ears.

Helios sighed. He had to keep his promise—and the time for his daily journey had already arrived. Harnessed and waiting, the horses were snorting impatiently. Dawn, his rosy-fingered sister, had already flung wide the gates of day.

Reluctantly Helios led Phaëthon to his waiting chariot and placed the reins in his son's hands. "You must always keep the horses in control," he warned sternly. "If they leave the path, terrible things will happen to heaven and earth—and to you. The ferocious beasts of the zodiac—the scorpion, the lion, the bull—wait above. They will attack if you lose control. It will certainly mean your death."

Phaëthon nodded, but his golden eyes were already on the sky as he embraced his sad-faced father. Helios set the crown of light on his son's head and commanded the horses to go forth. They leaped away through the gates of dawn, filling the sky with light. "Be careful!" he called.

Phaëthon felt such pride and excitement as the horses galloped into the sky that he thought his heart would burst. Driving the sun chariot was everything he had dreamed it would be.

But before long, the horses realized they had a new driver. The chariot was much lighter and easier to pull; the hands on the reins were less firm and sure. The horses began to run faster and faster, and soon they were out of control. The chariot swayed from side to side. The reins were whipped out of Phaëthon's hands, and then he could only clutch at the chariot, hanging on for dear life.

The horses galloped off their set path and ran wild through the houses of the zodiac. The savage beasts of the zodiac lashed out at Phaëthon with fang and claw. The panic-stricken horses plunged toward the earth, carrying the sun's flaming heat with them. They scorched the forests and fields, and set the mountainsides ablaze. The flames and smoke rose up, choking Phaëthon and burning him with their terrible heat until he wished he were dead.

Mother Earth herself could no longer bear the heat and cried out to the gods to help her. Zeus, looking down through the smoke that had risen up to Olympus, saw what had gone wrong. There was only one solution. Reluctantly he called for his lightning bolts.

Zeus hurled a bolt at Phaëthon in the careening chariot. It struck the boy dead and blasted the chariot apart. Phaëthon tumbled from the sky into the mysterious River Eridanus, which no mortal had ever seen.

The wreckage of the chariot and the sun's horses plunged into the sea. Hephaestus was forced to work all night, to repair the chariot in time for the new day. Poseidon sadly returned the exhausted horses to grieving Helios.

The naiads of the River Eridanus pitied Phaëthon, who had been so brave and died so young, and buried him beside the river. On his tomb they wrote, "He failed greatly, but only because he dared greatly."

Phaëthon's sisters, the Heliades—the daughters of Helios—mourned for him beside his grave. They wept for so long that at last the gods, in sympathy, turned them into poplar trees. Their golden tears, falling into the river, hardened into drops of amber, the golden jewels of the sun.

PEGASUS AND BELLEROPHON

Bellerophon was a son of Glaucus, the king of Corinth. Glaucus was a skilled horseman, but he fed his horses human flesh to make them fierce in battle. This offended the gods so much that one day they caused him to tumble from his chariot. His own horses devoured him.

Bellerophon was also an excellent horseman, but he was as kind as his father was cruel. It was whispered that he was not really Glaucus' son, but the son of Poseidon, who also loved horses.

Once while he was out hunting, Bellerophon looked up and saw Pegasus flying by. Pegasus was the silver-white winged horse who had sprung from the Gorgon Medusa's blood. He was the most beautiful horse Bellerophon had ever seen. The thought of taming Pegasus and riding him through the heavens filled Bellerophon's heart with longing. He would give anything to have a horse like that!

Bellerophon went to old Polyidus, the wisest man in Corinth, who could foresee the will of the gods. Bellerophon begged Polyidus to tell him how he could capture Pegasus.

"Even I am not wise enough to tell you that," Polyidus said. "You must go to Athena's temple and ask her."

That night Bellerophon went to Athena's temple and lay down to sleep, for the gods often spoke to people in their dreams. He dreamed that Athena stood before him, glowing with an unearthly light. "Are you sleeping?" she asked. "Wake up! Here is the thing that will win Pegasus." She held something golden in her hand.

Bellerophon woke with a start and looked around him. There was no goddess to be seen, only the quiet marble hall of the temple.

But then he saw something shining on the floor in the light of dawn. It was a golden bridle. Filled with hope, he picked it up and hurried out into the fields.

Nearby was a spring where Pegasus often came to drink. Bellerophon waited there, and soon the winged horse came fluttering down out of the sky, as graceful as any swan. Pegasus folded his wings and dipped his muzzle in the cool water.

Bellerophon approached the winged horse slowly, with soothing words. He held the golden bridle out in front of him. Pegasus lifted his head. With calm, dark eyes he watched Bellerophon approach and did not attempt to fly away. Athena's charm had worked. Pegasus let Bellerophon slip the bridle over his head and then climb onto his back.

Bellerophon could hardly believe that he was sitting astride this proud, beautiful creature. Pegasus vaulted into the air, his wings beating powerfully as he carried Bellerophon up toward the clouds. Pegasus obeyed Bellerophon's every command, swooping and soaring. They explored the sky together for hours, and Pegasus seemed to enjoy their new friendship as much as his rider did.

It was fortunate that the winged horse and his rider had formed such a bond, for Bellerophon would need Pegasus' help often in the future. Dangerous days lay ahead of him.

When Bellerophon paid a visit to King Proetus of Argos, the king became jealous of him. Proetus' wife seemed much too fond of the handsome prince with the famous flying steed. Proetus did not dare to harm Bellerophon, because Bellerophon was his guest. Like everyone, Proetus knew how the gods punished a treacherous host.

So Proetus came up with a deadly plan. He gave Bellerophon a letter and asked him to carry it to the king of Lycia, in Asia. The letter told the king of Lycia to kill whoever handed it to him. Bellerophon had no idea of this and was happy to take the letter there. A long journey was not difficult for him—it was a pleasure.

Bellerophon swung up onto Pegasus' back and flew away. When they reached Lycia, Bellerophon gave the king the letter immediately. The king put it aside. He was much more interested in Pegasus and the youth who had tamed him. The king quickly forgot about the letter and invited Bellerophon to stay with him for a time.

Nine days passed before the king remembered the letter. When he broke its seal and opened it at last, he was stunned. How could he possibly kill Bellerophon, who was now a welcome guest in his house?

But the king of Argos was a powerful friend. The king of Lycia did not want Proetus to become an enemy. He decided to send Bellerophon on a dangerous quest, hoping that he would be killed somewhere far from the palace.

The king told Bellerophon of the Chimera, a monster with the head of a lion, the body of a goat, and the tail of a serpent. It lived in the mountains nearby and had long ravaged Lycia. The king asked Bellerophon to slay the monster, knowing that many men had tried, but none had ever returned from the quest. He was sure that Bellerophon would never return either. But Bellerophon, who was young and full of courage, eagerly accepted the challenge. He and Pegasus flew off into the mountains.

Among the dark, jagged peaks he found the Chimera's lair.

Pegasus vaulted into the air, his wings beating powerfully...

...as he carried Bellerophon up toward the clouds.

The beast bellowed furiously as it saw him flying over its head. Flames roared out of its fanged jaws, and it raked the sky with its claws.

Riding on Pegasus' back, Bellerophon did not have to get near the flames. He circled over the Chimera like a taunting fly, always just beyond its reach. He fired arrow after arrow into its writhing body. At last its fuming rage ceased, and its body tumbled down, lying still among the rocks.

After telling the astonished king of Lycia that the Chimera was dead, Bellerophon flew back to King Proetus, to report that he had delivered the letter. Proetus was struck speechless for a moment, then thanked him gruffly. Proetus tried sending Bellerophon out on other dangerous errands, but the youth always returned triumphant, on the back of his shining-winged steed. Each time he became a greater hero.

At last even Proetus was won over by Bellerophon's earnestness and courage. He no longer felt jealous of the fortunate youth. They became true friends, and in time Bellerophon married one of Proetus' daughters.

Bellerophon lived happily in Argos for a long time. But at last he grew too proud of his unique steed and his own widening fame. He decided that he deserved to be on Olympus, among the gods. One day, while he was out flying, he tried to force Pegasus to carry him up to Olympus.

For the first and last time, Pegasus rebelled against Bellerophon's orders. He was wiser than his rider; he bucked Bellerophon off his back. Bellerophon fell a long, long way to the ground. Pegasus would no longer come at his call; the spell and their friendship had ended forever. Bellerophon wandered the earth for the rest of his life, alone and embittered, with no friend among mortals or gods.

Pegasus went on to a happier ending. For his wisdom in refusing Bellerophon's order, Zeus gave Pegasus a place in his royal stables. The winged horse became the favorite among all of Zeus' splendid creatures. Pegasus, with his thundering hooves striking sparks among the clouds, held the honor of bringing Zeus lightning and thunder when he had need for them.

ORPHEUS AND EURYDICE

The gods were the earliest musicians. Hermes invented the lyre, a kind of harp fashioned from tortoiseshell, which he gave to Apollo. Apollo played it so beautifully that the gods would stop whatever they were doing in the halls of Olympus to listen. Hermes also invented the shepherd's pipes, on which he made beautiful music himself. Pan, the forest god, made a pipe out of reeds. Athena invented the flute, although she never played it, because she thought it made her look undignified. The Muses did not play instruments, but the choir of their voices brought joy to all who heard them sing.

Next to the gods, a youth named Orpheus was the most skilled and talented musician who had ever lived. His mother was one of the Muses. His father was a prince of Thrace, the most music-loving land in Greece. When Orpheus sang and played his lyre, even the wild creatures of the forest came to sit silently and peacefully together, so they could hear his song. The very rocks and stones would move to hear him, and streams would change their course.

Orpheus fell in love with a young woman named Eurydice. His love for her inspired him so that his music was even more beautiful than before. They were married one warm summer day, and Orpheus was sure they would be happy together all their lives.

Then tragedy struck. As Eurydice walked through the

meadow at their wedding feast, a poisonous snake bit her on the heel. She died almost instantly.

Orpheus was frantic with grief. He loved Eurydice more than life itself. How could she be stolen away from him when their life together had just begun? It must be a mistake, he thought. He vowed to go down into the underworld to bring her back.

Because of his music and his great love for his wife, he was able to achieve what few mortals ever dared. He made his way down the dark passage that led beneath the earth, and the music he played touched grim old Charon so that he took Orpheus across the River Styx without complaint.

Cerberus, the Hound of Hell, lay down and wagged his barbed tail when he heard Orpheus play, and the vengeful Furies wept with remorse, for the first and last time.

At last Orpheus reached the throne where cold, unsmiling Hades sat with his bride, Persephone. Orpheus sang them a song of his love for Eurydice. In it he reminded Hades of the love the lord of the dead had once felt, a love so powerful that it had made him steal Persephone away from the world of the living. "You always win our souls, in the end," he sang. "But Eurydice's has come to you too soon." He asked only to borrow her back, he told Hades. When their full lives had been lived, they would both return forever.

Orpheus' music moved even the cold, pitiless heart of Hades. The lord of the underworld shed tears of iron and nodded his head. He called Eurydice to him. She came, a pale, whispering shadow. "Eurydice may return with you to the land of the living," Hades said, his deep voice echoing. "She will follow behind you up into the light. You must have faith in my word. If you doubt me and look back before you both reach the light, she will be lost to you. Forever."

Orpheus nodded. He turned away from the wan ghost of his beloved, although it was hard to tear his gaze from her. He started back up the long, dark path that led to the living world.

Orpheus kept walking, but as he walked he was filled with doubts. Why had Hades told him not to look back? Was it a trick? Was Eurydice really following him? He listened for the sound of her footsteps—but surely ghosts' feet made no sound. Would she really be the same?

Finally Orpheus saw light ahead. He ran out into the sunlit field and turned back at last. But he turned too quickly. Eurydice had not yet stepped into the light.

She raised her hands, reaching out to him. Already she was beginning to fade away. "Farewell," she whispered, and then she was gone.

"No—!" Orpheus cried in anguish. He ran back to the entrance of the underworld, but the gods would not let him pass inside again. He turned away, weeping, and fled into the hills.

Orpheus wandered through the wilderness of Thrace, grieving and alone. He would sit and play his music for hours, singing laments for his lost love. Even the stones wept to hear of his sorrow.

Then one day as he sat beside a river, he met a band of maenads. The women who followed Dionysus came shrieking through the forest in one of their wine-mad frenzies. They demanded that Orpheus join in their wild revels and play merry music so that they could dance. Orpheus could not, for he was so filled with grief.

The maenads, mad with fury, attacked him and tore him limb from limb. They hurled the pieces of his body into the river.

His head drifted downstream, still singing, to the astonishment of all who heard it from the shore. It was carried out to sea, to wash up on the island of Lesbos. His grieving mother and the other Muses buried it there, in a sanctuary. They placed his limbs in a tomb at the foot of Mount Olympus, and from that day on the nightingales sang more sweetly there than anywhere else on earth.

Orpheus' soul journeyed to the underworld, to be reunited forever with his beloved Eurydice.

JASON AND THE GOLDEN FLEECE

The story of the Golden Fleece actually begins years before the birth of its hero, Jason. It starts in Thessaly, with a king named Athamas. Tiring of his queen, he divorced her and took a princess named Ino as his new wife. Ino was a daughter of the famous King Cadmus of Thebes. Her mother and sisters were all well loved for their kindness. Ino was the exception in that good family.

Athamas and his first wife had two children, a son and a daughter. His first wife, the former queen, was afraid that Ino would try to kill her children, so that Ino's own child would be the next king. She was right. Ino ruined the grain harvest by secretly parching the kingdom's stored seed so that it would not grow. Soon the people had almost nothing to eat. They thought the gods were angry with them. The king sent a messenger to ask the oracle at Delphi what to do.

Ino bribed the messenger to say that the gods demanded the sacrifice of the king's children. The people forced him to agree to it, for they were starving. The king was very upset, because he loved his children. Still, he felt he must obey the gods.

The children, a boy named Phrixus and his little sister, Helle, were taken to the altar of a temple to be sacrificed. But then, miraculously, a ram with fleece of pure gold appeared. Zeus had sent the ram. He did not like human sacrifice, and he wanted to show the people that this was not what the gods had asked for.

The children climbed onto the ram's back, and it flew away with them.

The ram flew on and on, carrying the children toward safety. But after a time, as they were flying over the sea from Greece to Asia, Helle grew tired and lost her hold. She fell from the ram's back into the sea. Ever since, the sea has been called the Hellespont—Helle's Sea.

Phrixus clung to the ram's back until at last it came down in a land called Colchis, far to the east by the Black Sea. The people of Colchis did not welcome strangers. But Phrixus' arrival was so miraculous that they treated him very kindly. Grateful for his rescue, Phrixus sacrificed the golden ram to Zeus. (He knew it was no ordinary sheep and had to be returned to the gods.) From that time on, its golden fleece hung on a sacred tree, guarded by a dragon.

Jason's own story begins many years later. Jason was heir to the throne of Thessaly. But the kingdom had been stolen from Jason's father by Jason's uncle Pelias. Jason was sent away in secret to a place where he would be safe. There the wise centaur Chiron was his teacher as he grew up.

Meanwhile, the usurper, Pelias, spent years fearing that he would be killed by one of his relatives. He had asked an oracle to tell him what to watch out for. "Beware of a man with one shoe," the oracle said. Pelias ordered his soldiers to keep watch for such a person. Because he felt guilty, he worried constantly and had nightmares about the prediction.

When Jason was grown, he decided to claim the throne that was his by right. On his journey toward his father's city, he came one day to a wide river. An old woman sat forlornly on its bank. Jason greeted her politely and asked what he could do for her. He did not know it, but the old woman was Hera in disguise. She had come to watch over Jason's travels, and to see whether he was worthy of the gods' protection. "Please help me, sir," she said in a cracked, feeble voice. "I'm afraid to cross this river by myself."

Jason took her up on his back and waded into the river. The current was very swift and deep. Carrying the weight of an old woman who was really a goddess, Jason just barely managed to struggle across. His feet sank into the mud, and he lost one of his sandals before he reached the shore.

He left the old woman on the riverbank. She thanked him gratefully. He went on his way, never suspecting that he had won the favor of the gods.

Jason reached the city at last. The handsome, well-dressed youth with long golden hair was noticed by everyone. "Can he be Apollo?" people whispered. "Or the beloved of a goddess?" But the king's guards saw only a man wearing just one shoe—the man King Pelias had ordered them to watch out for. They sent for Pelias immediately.

When Pelias came to the market square, Jason stood calmly waiting for him. Pelias stared at Jason's bare foot, trying to hide his terror. "Where is your homeland, stranger?" Pelias asked. "Tell me the truth, now."

"This is my home," Jason answered. "I have come to right a wrong done to my family and restore our honor. I am your nephew Jason. The kingdom should be mine. But I did not come here to cause more grief by fighting you. Keep all your wealth, your cattle, and land. Only give me your crown and the right to rule. Then justice will be done."

Pelias was silent for a moment, thinking. Then he said, "All right. I agree. I am growing older, and this land needs a strong young man like you to rule it. But first"—and here he smiled— "there is something that must be done. There is a golden fleece that hangs in faraway Colchis. It belongs to our people—it was a gift from Zeus to us. The gods want it returned to its proper home. Bring it back, and you will prove that you deserve to be king."

Excitement filled Jason at the thought of such a journey. No one had ever attempted to sail all the way to the Black Sea from Greece. To go to that distant, barbaric land and bring back the Golden Fleece would be very dangerous—and a wonderful adventure. "I will do it gladly!" he said.

In front of his people Pelias swore by all the gods that he would give his kingdom to Jason when Jason returned. But he was sure that he would never have to keep his promise. Jason would certainly be lost or killed on his quest for the fleece.

Jason sent out messengers through all of Greece, calling the greatest heroes in the land to join him. He asked Hercules, the strongest man alive; Hercules' brave and clever cousin Theseus; the twins Castor and Pollux; Orpheus, famous for his musical skill; and many others. They all agreed to join him in his quest.

Before that time, the ships the Greeks built had always been very small. They could not carry many men or travel very far over unknown seas. Jason went to the famous shipbuilder Argus and asked him to design a new kind of ship, one that could make such a journey. Argus did. Jason named the ship the *Argo* in his honor, and the gathered heroes called themselves the Argonauts. Athena gave them a piece of magic wood for the ship's prow, to show the gods' favor. After making many offerings to thank the gods, the heroes set sail at last. Poseidon smiled on them and sent a strong wind to start them swiftly on their way.

On their journey eastward they stopped at Lemnos, an island where only women lived. The men of Lemnos had treated their wives, mothers, and children so badly that finally the women had risen up and driven them off the island. Now, seeing a strange ship approaching, the women put on their ex-husbands' armor and came down to the harbor, ready to defend their home. But Jason's messenger spoke to them politely, explaining the *Argo*'s mission and the noble ancestry of the heroes on board. All they asked, he told the women, was to take on some supplies.

The women, who had begun to wonder how they could go on raising families without husbands, asked the heroes to come ashore. They prepared a great feast and invited the Argonauts—the handsomest young men in Greece—to stay on Lemnos and become their new husbands. Even Jason, to whom the queen had proposed, was very tempted by the offer.

But Hercules, who had been left to guard the ship, grew impatient. He came ashore and found the Argonauts dawdling there. He drove them back aboard the ship with his club and told them sternly to remember their duty and the honor of their homeland.

When they set out again, the favorable wind had died down. The Argonauts took to their oars and began to row. Orpheus played stirring songs on his lyre to inspire them. Soon they began a contest to see who was the strongest rower.

One by one the Argonauts gave up their oars, exhausted. At last only Hercules and Jason himself were still in the contest. Finally even Jason collapsed, unable to take another stroke. Just at that moment Hercules' oar broke. Much to Hercules' disgust, the contest was a tie.

The Argonauts put ashore at a small island, to find wood to make another oar. While they worked, Hercules' young friend and armor bearer, Hylas, went to a spring to fill a jug with fresh water. As he bent over the pool, the nymph who lived there saw the handsome boy and fell in love with him. Reaching up with cool, silvery arms, she drew him down into the pool. He vanished without a trace.

When Hylas did not return to the ship, Hercules went searching for him. Hercules could not find Hylas anywhere, but he refused to stop searching. His distress at losing his friend drove him into one of his frequent fits of madness. He ran through the forest, shouting Hylas' name and smashing down anything in his path. Even the brave Argonauts were afraid of his blind fury and could do nothing. Reluctantly they sailed away without him.

Sailing farther east, the Argonauts reached the island of a wise king named Phineus. Apollo had given Phineus the ability to predict the future. This skill had made Zeus angry. The king of the gods did not like mortals who could predict his activities, especially since his activities usually made his wife so furious.

Zeus had sent hideous creatures called Harpies—birdlike monsters with women's heads—to torment Phineus. When Jason and the Argonauts arrived at the island, they found the king so weak that he could barely stand. He looked like a walking ghost, for he was slowly starving to death. Whenever he tried to eat, the horrid Harpies would fly down out of the sky and devour his food. Whatever they left was so fouled by their disgusting smell that he could not bear to eat it. No one in his country could protect him. Only someone as swift as the Harpies themselves could chase them away. As it happened, the heroes he needed were among the crew of the *Argo*—Zetes and Calais, the winged sons of the North Wind. He pleaded with them for help.

The Argonauts waited with Phineus as more food was set out. Phineus picked up a piece of meat. Swifter than thought the Harpies roared down out of the sky, in a terrible, shrieking, flapping mass. The Argonauts choked at the stench of them, but fought them off. As the Harpies fled, Zetes and Calais flew after them. They beat the Harpies so badly that they never came back.

The king was so grateful that he could not do enough for the Argonauts. He held an enormous banquet in their honor. As they ate, he told them how to avoid the perils that they would face on their way to Colchis.

The entrance to the Black Sea seemed impossible to pass through. It was guarded by the Symplegades, the Clashing Rocks. They crashed into each other constantly, while the sea boiled around them. "You must take a dove with you," Phineus said. "Let it go when you reach the rocks. If it flies through safely, you will get through safely, too. If it does not get through, turn back or you will surely die."

The Argonauts thanked him and went on their way. They took a dove with them and released it when they reached the place of the Clashing Rocks. The white water churned so wildly that it was hard even to keep their ship steady. The sound as the rocks crashed together was like thunder. The dove flew straight between the rocks as they pitched apart. It soared out the other side to safety just as they crashed together again. It lost only a few feathers from its tail.

"Quickly!" Jason shouted as the rocks rebounded, opening up again. "Row for your lives! Row!"

The Argonauts strained at the oars, and the *Argo* shot through the passage. They were safe—but they heard wood splinter as the ornament on the stern of their ship was crushed between the fangs of stone. Like the dove, they had barely escaped death. Looking back, they saw to their amazement that the rebounding rocks stood open now. The sea calmed, even as they watched, and the Clashing Rocks, now conquered, never moved again.

The Argonauts sailed on into the Black Sea, which was at that time called the Unfriendly Sea, because people living there hated strangers. The Argonauts passed the land of the Amazons—the famous women warriors—but this time they were not tempted to go ashore. The Amazons were descended from the nymph Harmony and Ares, the god of war. They followed their father's ways more eagerly than their mother's. The *Argo* sailed past the Caucasus Mountains, and the Argonauts saw Prometheus chained to his rock, with the vulture swooping down to attack him. They passed an island where cannibals lived.

At last, just at sunset of another day, they reached the land of Colchis. They camped for the night, feeling uncertain and very lonely. They were so far from home that they were not even sure the gods could hear their prayers. King Aeetes of Colchis was a son of Helios, the sun god. He killed all travelers who landed on his shores. The people of Colchis did not like foreigners any better than the Greeks themselves generally did.

Up on Olympus, Hera worried about the Argonauts' safety. So she went to Aphrodite and asked the goddess of love to help her protect them. King Aeetes had a beautiful daughter called Medea. She was golden-eyed like her father and all of Helios' descendants, and a priestess of Hecate, the goddess of moonless nights and witches. Hera knew Medea was a skilled sorceress. She asked Aphrodite to make Medea fall in love with Jason and use her magic to help him.

Aphrodite agreed. She told her little son, Eros, that she would give him a golden ball enameled with blue if he would shoot one of his arrows at Medea and cause her to fall in love.

The next morning Hera shrouded Colchis in fog, so that Jason and the Argonauts could make their way to Aeetes' palace without being attacked. When they appeared at his gates, his startled guards, discovering a group of well-dressed, noble-looking strangers, called for the king.

Finding the Argonauts already on his doorstep, Aeetes was forced to welcome them as guests. Even in wild Colchis, the gods frowned on anyone who failed to welcome guests kindly. Princess Medea stood looking on as the Argonauts entered. The moment she saw Jason, Eros' shaft struck her heart. She blushed as red as a rose and fell suddenly, utterly in love with the handsome foreigner. Frightened and amazed by the feeling, she hurried away to her room.

After his guests had eaten, the king at last asked who his visitors were, and why they had come. Jason introduced himself and his companions. He told Aeetes that they were all the sons or grandsons of the gods and that they had come to return the Golden Fleece to Greece. Jason promised that if Aeetes allowed them to take the Fleece, they would perform any deeds of strength or courage the king required.

King Aeetes was enraged by Jason's words. He felt that the Fleece had been given to his people by the gods. To him, the Greeks were no better than thieves. *If they had not eaten my food,* he thought, *I would kill them all.* But he hid his anger and said, "I shall be glad to give you the Golden Fleece if you can perform this feat. You must harness my two brass-footed, fire-breathing bulls and plow a field with them. You must sow the field with dragon's teeth. From each tooth a warrior will spring up. You must defeat them all. I have done this myself, and I will not give up the Fleece to anyone less strong or brave than I."

All the Argonauts stopped eating and stared at him. Even Jason was speechless when he heard what he must do. But he could not back down now. "All right," he said quietly. "I will do it tomorrow. You promise to give us the Fleece?"

"Of course," said Aeetes with an evil smile. No one had ever done what he asked Jason to do—not even Aeetes himself.

Jason and the Argonauts went back to their ship for the night. The heroes argued for hours, each of them asking Jason to let him take his place. He refused. "This was my idea," he said firmly. "If anyone must die, it will be me."

Meanwhile, Medea, who had overheard her father's plan, sat in her room, confused and unhappy. She knew she could use her magic to help Jason win the Fleece—but how could she betray her father and her people? She longed to be held in Jason's arms more than she wanted to be with her own family. She couldn't bear to think of him dead. *Why do I feel like this?* she wondered.

But she knew that she had already made up her mind—she would help Jason, no matter what. She called her favorite nephew to her and sent the boy to Jason's ship, to ask him to meet with her secretly.

Jason was very surprised to hear that the king's daughter, whom he had barely seen, wanted to help him. But at this point, he was happy for any aid.

He went back along the road to the palace with Medea's nephew. Medea was waiting for him. She had gone to the temple of Hecate and asked the goddess to show her how to save the man she loved. Jason saw Medea's golden eyes shining in the moonlight and suddenly felt that he had never seen anyone so beautiful.

Jason looked as handsome as Medea had remembered, like a young god. They stood together for a long moment, all smiles but suddenly too shy to speak.

Then Medea gave Jason a jar of magic salve that she had made. "If you rub this on yourself and on your weapons," she said, "you will be protected from iron and fire for one day. When the dragon warriors attack you, pick up a stone and throw it among them. They will turn and fight each other." She looked down and added, "When you are safely home in Greece, remember me, as I will always remember you."

Jason took the jar of salve. "I will never forget you!" he said. "If you come back with me to Greece, the people will honor you like a goddess. You and I will never be apart, night or day."

She shook her head. "I cannot help loving you," she said as tears filled her eyes. "But I also love my home and family. I cannot leave them." She turned and hurried back to the palace, weeping because she had betrayed her father, as her heart had betrayed her.

Jason returned to his ship alone and full of regret. He rubbed a fingerful of Medea's salve on his skin. He felt its power tingle through him and knew that she had told him the truth. When he explained what had happened, the other Argonauts were filled with wonder and relief. Jason carefully rubbed the ointment all over himself and his weapons.

The next morning the Argonauts went back to Aeetes' palace. Jason walked boldly out into the field where Aeetes and his people stood waiting. The bulls were let out of their stable and came thundering across the field. Their brazen hooves shook the earth. They bellowed and snorted fire. Even knowing that Jason had a magic charm, the Argonauts trembled in terror at the sight of the beasts. Medea, who knew she had protected Jason as well as anyone could, still held her breath in fear and said a prayer to Hecate.

His heart beating fast, Jason stood his ground as the bulls approached. He felt the strength of Medea's potion protecting him, and the fiery breath of the bulls did not burn him. He forced one and then the other to their knees and yoked them to a plow. And then he plowed the field with them, scattering dragon's teeth in the furrows.

Even before he had finished plowing, armed men began to spring up out of the fresh-turned earth. The warriors ran at him, shouting and waving their swords.

Jason dropped the plow and drew his own sword. He fought heroically, but there were dozens of them against one, and he was overwhelmed by their numbers. Then he remembered what Medea had told him. He grabbed a rock and flung it into the ranks of warriors.

Forgetting Jason, they turned furiously on one another and fought until they were all dead. The Argonauts cheered, and Medea felt weak with relief.

Instead of congratulating Jason, Aeetes turned and stalked off the field. Again he was filled with rage, this time because Jason had accomplished his task. "The Greeks are nothing but barbarians," he muttered. He swore that they would never have the Golden Fleece—he would kill them first.

That night Medea overheard her father's secret plans. Torn with anguish and love, she decided that she must warn Jason and run away with him—for she could never stay here after saving the Argonauts. Wrapping a midnight-colored cloak around her, she hurried to his ship.

When Jason came out to see her, she cried, "My father means to kill you all! You must take the Fleece and go—now! I will help you, but you must take me with you also, for he will never forgive me!" She sank to the ground and began to weep as thoughts of her lost home filled her.

Jason lifted her up gently and told her she would have a new home now, with him. He promised that she would be his wife as soon as they reached Greece. They hurried aboard the *Argo* and set sail down the river to the place where the Fleece was kept.

A huge dragon lay coiled around the sacred tree where the Fleece hung, guarding it. But Medea waved Jason and his sword aside. The young sorceress walked fearlessly through the moonlight toward the dragon. She sang as she went, and her magic song lulled the monster to sleep. Jason took the Fleece from the tree, and they hurried on their way.

When Aeetes discovered what had happened, he called out his army. He sent his ships after the *Argo*, with Medea's brother Apsyrtus leading them. The army was huge, and the Colchian warships were so fast the *Argo* could not outrun them.

Again Medea helped the Argonauts. She sent a message to her brother, telling him that she had been kidnapped and wanted to be rescued. When he came to find her on the shore, Jason was waiting for him. They fought, and Jason killed Apsyrtus.

The Colchian fleet was forced to turn back so that King Aeetes could give the prince a proper funeral. The Argonauts sailed away swiftly. But now the gods were angry, for Medea had caused her own brother's death. Poseidon sent a furious storm to catch the *Argo* at sea. Zeus' lightning bolts split the sky. The Argonauts were certain that the *Argo* would sink, and they would all die.

Then the magical piece of wood in the prow, which had been given to them by Athena herself, spoke to the Argonauts. It told them that the only way they could save themselves was to seek out the sorceress Circe. They had to ask her to purify Medea and Jason of their sin. Circe was famous for her fearsome magic, but she also happened to be Medea's aunt. Because of that, there was hope that she would help them.

The *Argo* fought its way through the mountainous waves of the storm-tossed sea. At last it reached Circe's island, off the shore of what is now Italy.

Circe was no friend to men. She felt that most men behaved like animals, and that was what she turned them into with her magic spells. Medea warned the Argonauts to stay on their ship, where they would be safe. Then, taking Jason by the hand to protect him, she led the way to Circe's palace.

Circe, who was also a descendant of Helios, knew her niece instantly by the golden eyes that matched her own. A powerful sorceress, she also knew of Medea's plight. She did not like the fact that Medea had gotten into such trouble for love of a man. Still, she felt sympathy for the forlorn girl and her weary beloved.

Circe agreed to make the proper sacrifices and say the proper prayers to the gods, asking their forgiveness. The sound of her words was carried up to Zeus on the smoke scented with rich meat and fragrant herbs. Her words soothed his anger, and he relented. "You are forgiven," he rumbled. He waved his hand, and the seas calmed at last. Jason and Medea hurried back to their ship. Circe watched the *Argo* sail away and shook her head.

The Argonauts were overjoyed to be sailing homeward. But they had gone far out of their way to reach Circe's island, and they still had to pass through waters as dangerous as the ones they had faced on their journey to Colchis.

They sailed near the rocks where the Sirens sang. The Sirens, enchantresses with beautiful voices, often lured sailors overboard with their haunting songs. But this time Orpheus played his lyre, drowning out their fatal voices with his music, and the Argonauts sailed past in safety.

Then Scylla and Charybdis loomed ahead. Scylla was a hideous monster with the upper body of a woman and six ferocious monster heads instead of limbs. She crouched below a sheer cliff beside the place where Charybdis lay. Charybdis' huge, ever-hungry mouth sucked water down into a vast whirlpool, which churned the sea and tossed waves sky-high, swallowing ships and their crews whole. To pass between Scylla and Charybdis seemed impossible. But Hera sent the sea nymphs called Nereids up from the depths to sweep the *Argo* safely through the passage.

When the exhausted Argonauts approached the island of Crete, Medea warned them to be wary. A bronze giant named Talus, who had been built by the inventor Daedalus, guarded the island. Every day Talus walked the perimeter of Crete, patrolling its shores. The indestructible metal man had only one weak spot, on his heel.

Even as Medea spoke, Talus appeared on the shore. He began to hurl huge boulders into the water, churning up waves that threatened to sink the *Argo*. Medea prayed to Hecate to save them. As if in answer to her prayers, the next time the giant lifted a rock, he slipped and cut his heel. His artificial blood gushed out of him, and he fell into the sea, dead. The Argonauts were finally able to land to take on food and water.

After a long, dangerous journey, the *Argo* reached Greece at last. The band of heroes said their farewells to one another with both joy and sorrow. Nothing, they were certain, would equal the adventure they had shared together.

Jason and Medea carried the Golden Fleece to Thessaly. But when they arrived, they learned that treacherous King Pelias had caused the death of Jason's father. Jason's mother had died soon

He began to hurl huge boulders into the water, churning up waves...

after of grief. Jason knew now that Pelias would never keep his word. The king would surely try to kill him, too.

Jason vowed revenge. Again he turned to Medea for help. Out of love for him, she devised a plan that would give him what he wanted. She went into the city, disguised as an old woman selling magic herbs. She went to Pelias and said, "I can show you how to become young again." Pelias was eager to believe her.

Medea asked to see his daughters. While Pelias' daughters watched, she cut up an old ram and put it into a pot of boiling water, along with magic herbs. She spoke a spell over the pot. Suddenly a young lamb leaped from it and gamboled away. Medea told Pelias' daughters that the same thing could happen for their father—but only they could grant his wish and make him young. She gave them a potion to put him to sleep, and magic herbs. They must do with him as she had done with the sheep, she said.

His daughters were frightened by the terrible prospect, but they did as she told them, for their father was old and sick, and longed to be young again. They put him into a pot with the magic herbs. But they did not know what spells to say, and their father did not leap from the pot, a young man again. Trusting Medea, they had killed him. Jason had his revenge.

Jason and Medea left the Golden Fleece in Thessaly and went to Corinth. They lived there for some years and had two sons. Though she missed her homeland, Medea loved Jason and their children, so she was content at first. Then Jason began to change. His longing for fame and glory returned, and in time it was all he could think about. He forgot the love and gratitude he had once felt for Medea. He decided to marry a princess of Corinth, so that he would become the next king.

When he told Medea he wanted to marry someone else, she was heartbroken and furious. The angry words she spoke to him then were carried back to the king of Corinth. He feared she would try to hurt his daughter. He told Jason that Medea and her children must leave Corinth forever.

Medea could not believe that Jason would let them be exiled. "Everything I did, I did for you!" she cried. "I saved your life again and again. My love for you made me do terrible things. How can you send me and your sons away? We will have no one to protect us or help us. We will die, or live as slaves. How can you be so cruel?"

Jason said coldly that he had never needed her help to be a hero. He did not need her now.

He left her there, and she felt her world had ended. In her grief and anger, she took a beautiful robe and soaked it in deadly poison. She sent it as a gift to Jason's intended wife, with a message of apology. The princess put it on and died. Medea had her revenge, but now she felt her life was over. She would sooner kill her sons and herself, she vowed, than suffer at the hands of cruel strangers—or suffer Jason's vengeance.

But Hera had grown very angry with Jason for breaking his vows to Medea. His behavior reminded her painfully of her own husband's fickle conduct. She took pity on Medea and appeared before her. "Give your sons to me," said Hera, "and I will make them immortal." She carried their souls up to Olympus with her. Then Helios, the all-seeing sun, golden-eyed Medea's grandfather, sent his blazing chariot down to her. She stepped into it, and the fiery horses swept her away from Corinth, away from Jason's piti-less anger at what she had done to his betrothed.

As he watched her go, he cursed her, never himself, for the loss of all he had.

Nothing ever went well for Jason again. Like so many heroes, he had outlived his heroism. He fled Corinth and the king's wrath to wander friendless from place to place, until at last he came upon the *Argo*. It lay beached and rotting on the strand where it had been abandoned, years before, after its voyage ended.

Jason lay down to rest in the shade of its bow. As he dozed there, dreaming of past glories, Athena's prow of sacred wood broke loose and fell on him, killing him. Thus ended the life of a man whom gods and mortals alike had once favored and had now forgotten. Only the Golden Fleece remained, hanging in the tem-ple of Apollo—a reminder of a grand adventure and better days.

ATALANTA

Atalanta, who lived at the same time as Jason and the other Argonauts, was as strong and swift and brave as any of them. Only one thing about Atalanta was different. Atalanta was a woman.

When Atalanta was born, her father was angry because, like most men of his time, he wanted a son, not a daughter. He ordered his baby daughter to be abandoned on a wild mountainside—a cruel fate that was not uncommon in those days.

Atalanta was found by a mother bear, who raised the baby as one of her own cubs. Atalanta grew into a swift, strong, wild little girl. One day she was discovered by two kind-hearted hunters who were out looking for game. They adopted her and took her home with them. As she grew older, Atalanta learned all their hunting skills, and soon was a better hunter than either of them.

One day when she was out alone in the woods, she came upon two centaurs. The wild half-human creatures came galloping toward her, ready to carry her off. She did not try to run—that would have been useless. She stood her ground and put an arrow in her bowstring. She shot one centaur, and then shot the other. Both of them collapsed at her feet, mortally wounded.

Some time after that, she heard that heroes from all over the land were being asked to go to Calydonia for a boar hunt. The king of Calydonia, Oeneus, had insulted Athena by forgetting her share of the offerings at the harvest festival. To punish him, Athena had sent a gigantic boar to run wild through his country, causing death and destruction everywhere. The boar was so ferocious that it had killed or wounded the bravest hunters in Calydonia; none had been able to stop it. Now King Oeneus had called on the greatest heroes in all of Greece to help him.

Atalanta's skill as a hunter was well known, so she was also invited. She arrived at the gathering place eager for the hunt to begin. Meleager, Oeneus' son, took one look at her and fell in love. To him she was like the goddess Artemis—whose ways she followed—in human form. Her hair was pulled back in a simple bun, and she was dressed like a man, in a short tunic. She wore no makeup or jewelry at all, but to Meleager's mind, those would only have spoiled her proud, perfect beauty.

Some of the other hunters gathered there did not view her the same way. They argued that it was insulting for men to hunt with a woman. But Meleager insisted, and they could not disagree with the king's son.

As it turned out, the hunters were lucky that Atalanta had joined them. Suddenly there came a tremendous crashing and snorting in the woods, and the Calydonian boar burst from the trees. Its attack was so sudden and fierce that it killed two hunters before anyone could move to strike back. In the confusion, a third hunter was accidentally killed by a spear that missed its mark.

Only Atalanta stood her ground and remained calm, as she had with the centaurs. She drew her bow and fired an arrow. It struck the boar. The boar, though not mortally wounded, staggered and slowed its attack. Meleager seized the chance to rush in and stab the beast with his spear, killing it.

Everyone ran forward to congratulate the prince. They skinned the boar and gave Meleager the hide. It was to be displayed as a tribute to his heroism. But Meleager insisted that Atalanta should be given the credit, and also the hide of the boar, because she had stopped the beast's ferocious attack and was the first to wound it. Atalanta accepted the hide and thanked Meleager for his generous gesture. It won him her respect, but not the love he would have preferred. And neither of them suspected the terrible price Meleager would pay for his gallantry.

The other visiting hunters resented his decision. They could not accept being outshone by a woman. None of them dared to object, however, since they were guests in Meleager's land.

But Meleager had two uncles, his mother's brothers, who were not held back by the rules of hospitality. They argued angrily with Meleager about his decision. Their tempers were already on edge because of the deaths that had occurred and the scare the boar had given them. Now Meleager's two uncles drew their swords and told him to change his mind or die. Meleager drew his own sword and fought with them. He killed them both.

The astonished witnesses quickly made their farewells and went on their way. If Meleager had hoped this act would win Atalanta's heart, he was wrong. Atalanta left too, after thanking him for defending her right to the prize. She was more certain than ever that she did not want to marry, after seeing how all the men around her at the hunt had behaved.

Meleager returned to his father's palace, alone and uncertain about what he had done. He never suspected that he was going home to his doom.

For what he did not know was the strange thing that had happened on the day he was born. The Fates had appeared to his mother, Queen Althea, and shown her a log in the fire. "Your son will live only until that branch has been completely burned," they said.

Meleager's mother, horrified, pulled the branch from the hearth and poured water on it. She hid the unburned piece of wood in a chest. It had lain there for years, and only she knew about it.

Now word was brought to her that her son had killed her beloved brothers. In a fit of grief and anger, she took the branch from its hiding place and threw it into the fire.

Meleager felt a burning pain inside him as the fire consumed the branch. He collapsed in the courtyard, clutching his chest. By the time the branch had burned to ashes, he was dead. His poor mother, aghast at what she had done, killed herself.

By this time, Atalanta was far away. She never knew of the tragedy she had unintentionally caused. She went on with her life of adventure. She asked to sail with Jason and the Argonauts on their voyage to find the Golden Fleece, but Jason talked her out of it. So she contented herself with performing daring deeds at home. After the Argonauts' return, at the funeral games of King Pelias, she won a wrestling match with the young hero Peleus, who would become the father of Achilles, one of the greatest heroes in the Trojan War.

She also learned who her real parents were and went to live with them. Her father, having heard of all her exploits, had decided that having a daughter was not so bad after all, and at long last welcomed her.

Atalanta continued to have many marriage proposals. At that time the ordinary Greek woman stayed at home, raised children, and obeyed everything her husband said. Even so, there were young men who admired that rare woman who was independent and chose her own way of life.

Atalanta still wanted nothing to do with any suitors, however. Too often it seemed as if they just wanted to marry her so that they could make her give up her free life and be their servant. She therefore told anyone who asked to marry her that he must run a race with her. If he won it, she would marry him. But of course no one in Greece was a faster runner than Atalanta, who had grown up with wild animals for companions. She always won.

Then a youth named Hippomenes came along. He knew that he was not stronger or faster than the woman he had fallen in love with. No one had ever beaten her in a race. He had to try something different. If strength couldn't win her, maybe cleverness could.

He went to the temple of Aphrodite and asked the goddess of love to help him win Atalanta's heart and win the race as well.

Aphrodite was always annoyed with young people who refused to fall in love. She felt that to be in love was the most wonderful thing in the world. So she told Hippomenes that she would help him. She gave him three apples made of gold. They were so beautifully made and so precious that no one could resist them.

Hippomenes carried the apples with him to the starting line of the race. Atalanta stood beside him, strong and proud, and he thought she had never seemed more beautiful. She looked at him and secretly thought that he was very handsome, too. They had spent a lot of time talking before he asked to marry her, and she found that she liked him in spite of herself. He was not as arrogant as the heroes she knew. But he did not look very fast. She was sure he would lose like all the rest.

The signal was given, and the runners burst from the starting line. Atalanta quickly began to pull ahead, though Hippomenes ran with all his might. He tossed out the first apple before she got too far ahead. It rolled in front of her, and she stopped to pick it up.

Hippomenes drew even with her, but in a flash she was ahead of him again. As they ran on across the field, he tossed out another apple. It rolled to one side, so that Atalanta had to swerve to pick it up. This time Hippomenes managed to get ahead of her, but she quickly outdistanced him again.

As they came toward the finish line, he tossed out the last apple. This time he pitched it as hard as he could. It rolled off into the woods. Atalanta darted after it, sure that she could claim the beautiful apple and still win the race. She picked the apple up and raced back toward the finish line.

But Hippomenes had put on a final burst of speed and pulled far ahead. Atalanta ran faster than she had ever run before—but it was too late. Hippomenes crossed the finish line a heartbeat ahead of her. The impossible had happened—someone else had won the race!

"Now you must keep your promise," Hippomenes said. "Will you take these golden apples, a gift from Aphrodite, as an engagement gift? Will you marry me?"

"That was hardly a fair race," said Atalanta. But she smiled. It pleased her that Hippomenes had used his imagination instead of simply his strength. Maybe he was someone truly worthy of her love. She looked at the golden apples in her hands. They were fit for a goddess. "I will keep my promise," she said. "I will be your wife. But I will never give up hunting!"

EROS AND PSYCHE

Once long ago in Greece there was a king who had three daughters. The youngest, Psyche, was the most beautiful. She outshone her sisters as the moon outshines the stars. People came from miles around to gaze at her and praise her, saying that she was more beautiful than the goddess Aphrodite herself.

Aphrodite became very jealous when she heard this. She called on her son, Eros, who was now full grown and the god of love. She told him to punish Psyche. "Strike her heart with one of your arrows," she said. "Make her fall in love with the most horrible, ugly thing alive."

But Eros, when he saw just how beautiful Psyche was, stood speechless. He felt, suddenly, as if one of his arrows had struck his own heart. His mother went away, sure that he would do what she had asked. She never suspected that Love himself had fallen in love.

Eros did not fire an arrow at Psyche; Psyche did not fall in love with anyone. And surprisingly, no one fell in love with her. They admired and praised her, but they married her less-pretty sisters. Psyche was so beautiful she frightened men. She grew sad and lonely.

Finally her father visited Apollo's oracle at Delphi. Eros had told Apollo of his secret love for Psyche, and Apollo had promised to help him. Apollo told the king that his daughter must be dressed as if she were going to her own funeral, and left on a nearby mountaintop. A monstrous dragon would come in the night and carry her off, he said. That was to be her fate.

Her father was speechless, and her sisters wept with sorrow. But Psyche said, "You should have pitied me before, because no one loved me. Now at least my loneliness will end."

She climbed bravely to her spot on the mountaintop. Her reluctant family left her there and went home to grieve for her. Psyche sat trembling in the darkness, listening for the sound of terrible wings. Instead there was only the sigh of a gentle breeze. The wind lifted her as if she were a cloud and carried her down into a peaceful valley. It left her there in a flower-filled meadow, beside a stream. She no longer felt afraid, but lay down and slept.

In the morning she woke to find a beautiful palace of silver and gold across the stream. Voices called to her, inviting her inside. This was to be her new home, they said. Psyche bathed and dressed in the beautiful robes laid out for her by unseen hands. Voices guided her to a delicious banquet. As she ate, an invisible choir sang sweetly.

That evening she went to bed, sure that her husband would come to join her there—and somehow sure that he was not at all horrible. He did join her, although she could not see him in the dark. His voice was so kind, and his words so loving, that she fell in love with him.

Her days and nights continued in this way. She had every-thing she could wish for by day, except her mysterious husband. They were together only at night. Psyche felt content and happy, if still a little lonely.

But one night in the darkness her husband said, "I must warn you of a danger. Your sisters are coming to the mountaintop to mourn for you. You must not go to see them, or you will make us both very unhappy."

When she heard this, Psyche began to cry. "I miss my sisters so much," she said. "Please let me have this one visit. I only want them to know that I'm safe and happy."

Her husband at last gave in. "You may have your visit," he said. "But remember that I warned you about this. And never, never try to see what I look like. If you do, you will lose me forever." Psyche promised him that she would never do such a thing.

The next morning the breeze carried her sisters down into the meadow. The three young women laughed and cried and hugged each other. They spent the rest of the day talking. Psyche showed them through her beautiful home and said that her husband was out hunting.

Her sisters' happiness for her faded, and they started to feel jealous of her good fortune. Then, because she could not describe him, they began to suspect that she really didn't know what her husband looked like. "Your husband treats you kindly now," they said. "But Apollo's oracle said he was a terrible monster. You should kill him as he sleeps, or one night he will surely kill you."

They left, and poor Psyche did not know what to think. She argued silently with herself all day about what she should do. When night came at last, her husband returned. Psyche had hidden a lamp and a knife near the bed. When her husband was asleep, she lit the lamp and picked up the knife.

Holding the lamp over his sleeping form, she found not a horrible monster, but the handsomest youth she had ever seen. She gasped in amazement and dropped the knife. But in her surprise she spilled a drop of hot lamp oil on Eros' shoulder.

He woke with a cry and saw her standing over him. Without a word he rose from the bed and rushed out into the night.

Holding the lamp over his sleeping form, she found...the handsomest youth she had ever seen.

Grief-stricken, Psyche called after him. The voice she knew so well answered her from the darkness, telling her that her husband had been Eros, the god of love. "Love cannot live where there is no trust," Eros' voice said sadly. And then the night was silent.

My husband was the god of love! thought Psyche. *And I was so foolish that I drove him away.* She vowed that instead of feeling sorry for herself, she would go in search of him. *Even if he doesn't love me anymore, I'll show him how truly I love him. I'll search forever, if I must.*

Meanwhile, Eros had gone home to his mother, Aphrodite. Aphrodite put a soothing ointment on his burn, but she was not very sympathetic. "You married that girl—a mere mortal yet! I told you to punish her!" Aphrodite said angrily. "You deserve what happened to you!" Eros was very glum and didn't even argue.

"Stay here in my palace until you're better," Aphrodite told him firmly. Then she went out to search for Psyche. She wanted to punish Psyche herself.

Meanwhile, Psyche had searched every place that she could think of for Eros. At last she decided to seek out Aphrodite and beg the goddess for forgiveness. She did not know Aphrodite was already looking for her. *Maybe Eros is with his mother,* she thought, *and I might at least see him.*

She went to Aphrodite's temple and prayed. Aphrodite appeared before her. "You have hurt my son. He does not want to see you ever again," Aphrodite said. "And furthermore, you have insulted me."

"I'll do anything to make up for it and win back Eros' love," Psyche said tearfully.

"Very well," Aphrodite said. She smiled cruelly. "You will be my servant, and do whatever I tell you to do. Then we'll see."

Aphrodite made heaps of grain appear on the ground outside her temple. The tiny kernels of barley, oat, and wheat whirled together into one big pile at a wave of her hand. "There," Aphrodite said. "Sort these out again by nightfall and put them in bags. If you fail, I will punish you." She left Psyche alone with her task.

Psyche's tears fell faster. She knew she could not possibly sort out all that grain by sunset.

But although Aphrodite felt no pity for her, the tiny ants creeping through the grass did. "Come," they whispered to one another, "let's help this poor unfortunate person. She doesn't deserve such treatment."

Psyche watched in amazement as thousands of ants swarmed over the heap of grain and sorted it into piles. She quickly put the grain into sacks. "Oh, thank you," she cried as the ants scurried away in a dark tide, just as the sun was setting.

When Aphrodite returned, she frowned in frustration. "How did you do that?" she said. "You must have had help!"

Psyche did not answer her. "Well, here," Aphrodite said. "You can have this bowl of barley gruel for supper, and sleep in the grass." Her footsteps left a trail of flowers as she went back inside her glowing temple for the night. Psyche was already thin and tired from her long travels and her unhappiness. Aphrodite thought secretly that if she made Psyche work hard enough and gave her little enough to eat, Psyche's famed beauty would fade. Then no one, not even Eros, would think Psyche was more beautiful than the goddess of love. Aphrodite made Psyche grind up grain for meal and scrub the floors of her temple while she thought up more difficult tasks.

"Go down to the river," Aphrodite said the next afternoon.

"Wild sheep with golden fleece come there to drink. Gather enough golden wool so that I can make a gown of it. If you fail, you will be punished."

The wild rams were very fierce, and Psyche was afraid they would attack her if she tried to pull out their wool. She sat by the riverbank, looking at her thin, weary reflection. She felt so sad that again she began to cry. She did not know what to do. She felt as if she might as well throw herself into the river and drown.

But the green reeds growing on the riverbank whispered softly, "Don't despair. When the wild sheep come to drink, they pass through the thornbushes beside the river. Their fleece gets caught on the thorns. You can gather all the wool you need."

Psyche waited all day until the wild sheep came butting and *baa*ing down to drink. When they had thundered away again, golden wool glittered everywhere in the bushes. She gathered it carefully and took it back to Aphrodite.

"Hmph!" Aphrodite said, tapping her foot. "You must have had help again." But she took the fleece and went back inside her temple.

The next day she sent Psyche to fetch a bottle of water from the River Styx, the dark river that guarded the way to the underworld. Psyche went to the place where the river sprang out of the ground in a torrent. The rocks around it were steep and slippery with moss. If she tried to climb over them, she would surely fall into the river and be swept away.

This time she was not afraid. Each time before, something had come to her aid. She knew that she was enduring these trials for the best of reasons—because she wanted to make up for her selfishness and doubt. Perhaps secretly the gods were on her side.

As she looked around her, an eagle suddenly swooped down out of the heights. The eagle took her bottle in its talons and flew away to fill it for her. With the bottle of Styx water in her hands, Psyche hurried back to find Aphrodite.

This time Aphrodite was ready with a task she was sure a mere mortal would fail at. She told Psyche to go to Persephone, the queen of the underworld, and ask her to send back some of her beauty in a box. "Tell her I'm worn out and haggard from caring for my poor wounded son," Aphrodite said venomously.

Again Psyche obeyed without complaining. As she went on her way, waiting for a sign, a voice spoke to her from an abandoned tower. It told her where to find an entrance to the underworld. "When you reach the River Styx, give Charon the ferryman a coin to carry you across," the voice said. "Go on to the gate where Cerberus waits. If you give him cakes to eat, he will let you go by."

Psyche did as she was told. She went down and down into the darkness until she found Charon. She gave him a coin, and he let her enter his boat. He ferried her across the Styx. She walked on until she met Cerberus. She tossed a cake to each of the hellhound's snarling heads. Cerberus lay down on the cold stone floor, wagging his spiked tail. Psyche went in through the adamantine gates, tiptoeing along the narrow path among the ghostly spirits toward Hades' midnight palace.

Knowing why Psyche had come, Persephone greeted her kindly and handed her a box. "Take this back to Aphrodite with my regards," Persephone said.

Psyche climbed the steep, dark path into the light again and continued on her way. But when she had almost reached Aphrodite's temple, she stopped. *I look so tired and worn,* she thought. *Perhaps if I used just a little of the beauty magic in this box myself...* She opened the box.

An enchanted sleep overcame her and she collapsed in the grass.

By this time Eros' wound had healed. He had forgiven his wife and missed her terribly. Aphrodite had locked him in his room so that he wouldn't see Psyche, but he flew out the window—it is hard to keep Love captive.

Determined to search for his wife, Eros soon found her asleep in the grass near Aphrodite's temple. He swept the enchanted-sleep dust back into its box and woke her with a kiss. She opened her eyes and was amazed and overjoyed to see her husband.

He held up his hand before she could speak. "You must take the box to my mother," he said. "Prove your dedication to her. Now that I've found you, everything will be all right." He gave her another kiss. Smiling, Psyche got to her feet and carried the box to Aphrodite.

Meanwhile, Eros flew up to Olympus and asked Zeus to help him set things right.

"You have made a fool of me many times, boy," Zeus said with a wry smile. "But I will help you. Maybe a wife will keep you out of mischief."

Hermes brought Psyche up to Olympus, where she was given ambrosia to eat. Eating the food of the gods made her an immortal. Aphrodite forgave Psyche at last, declaring that she was a suitable match for Eros.

Eros and Psyche—whose names mean *Love* and *Soul*—lived happily ever after.

THESEUS AND THE MINOTAUR

Aegeus, the king of Athens, met Aethra, the daughter of the king of Troezen, when he was traveling through her land. They fell in love and were married. When Aegeus had to return to Athens, Aethra was expecting a child. "Athens can be a dangerous place. There are always people who plot against a king, " he said. "Stay here with your father and raise our child in the peaceful countryside. That way you both will be safe and happy." He took his sword and a pair of fine sandals, and placed them beneath a heavy stone. "If our baby is a boy, bring him to this place," he told her. "When he is strong enough to move the stone aside, send him to me in Athens."

Aethra's baby was a boy, and she named him Theseus. He grew up tall and strong. Finally one day she took him to the place where his father's sword was hidden. He rolled the stone aside easily and claimed his inheritance—his father's sword and shoes.

His grandfather told him, "I have a ship ready to take you up the coast to Athens. It's too dangerous to travel overland alone. You'll get there safely by ship."

Theseus didn't want to be safe. He wanted to be a famous hero, like his cousin Hercules, the strongest man alive. He wanted his father to be proud of him when they met. He insisted on taking the inland road.

The dangerous road to Athens was filled with bandits and murderers. Though he traveled alone, Theseus walked the road fearlessly. He was attacked again and again, but each time he defeated the cutthroats and thieves he met.

At last Theseus reached Athens. Reports of his heroic deeds had reached the city before him, and he was welcomed by the people there. King Aegeus invited Theseus to a banquet, not realizing that the now-famous youth was his own son.

While Theseus was growing up in the peaceful land of his grandfather, Aegeus had married again. His new wife was the sorceress Medea, who had come to Athens after fleeing her husband Jason. Medea, through her sorcery, knew that Theseus was Aegeus' son. She also knew that her own influence as queen would be lost if Aegeus recognized this heroic young man as his son and heir. She did not want to be treated by Aegeus the way she had been treated by Jason.

So Medea went to Aegeus and convinced him that Theseus was dangerous—that he had come to Athens to steal Aegeus' throne. She urged Aegeus to give Theseus a cup of poisoned wine at the banquet.

Aegeus agreed. He asked Theseus to join him in drinking a toast at the banquet. But as Theseus came toward him across the hall, Aegeus suddenly saw that Theseus was wearing his own sword. He threw aside the poisoned cup and embraced his son. Medea, who was watching, saw the furious look Aegeus gave her. She fled into the night. Eventually she reached Asia, and settled in a land that bore her name for many centuries afterward.

Aegeus was delighted to have his son with him at last and proclaimed Theseus his heir.

But Theseus' happy homecoming in Athens was soon darkened by an event as sad as his arrival was joyous. Long years ago, Minos, the powerful ruler of Crete, had sent his son to visit Athens. Aegeus had unwisely let the boy join an exciting but dangerous hunt, and the boy had been killed. To repay the loss of Minos' son, Aegeus had been forced since then to send fourteen Athenians—seven young men and seven young women—to Crete every nine years. The fourteen unfortunate victims, who were chosen in a lottery, were sent into the Labyrinth, a maze of tunnels beneath Minos' palace. There the Minotaur—a monster half man and half bull—waited for them. None ever returned.

When Theseus heard of this, he quickly volunteered to be one of the fourteen young people. His father objected, but Theseus would not change his mind. "I'll stop this terrible curse or die trying," he said.

The ship that carried the victims to Crete always bore a black sail of mourning. Theseus ordered that a white sail be put on board. "When I succeed and we all come home, I will raise the white sail," he promised his father. "Then you will know as soon as you see the ship that we are alive."

The ship carried Theseus and the thirteen other young Athenians to the island of Crete. They were led to Minos' palace through streets lined with shouting, jeering Cretans.

Looking out from the palace walls was Ariadne, Minos' daughter. She felt her brother's death had been an accident and had always been troubled by her father's bitterness and cruelty toward the people of Athens. Now she looked down at the forlorn band of young Athenians coming toward the palace, and her heart went out to them. And then her eyes fell on Theseus. He was the handsomest youth she had ever seen, and she fell in love with him at first sight. She was determined to save him.

She went to Daedalus, the brilliant architect and inventor who had designed the Labyrinth. She pleaded with him to tell her how to save the young man she loved. Daedalus gave her a ball of string. "There is no way to learn the maze," he said. "But tell the young Athenian to fasten this to the door when they go inside. The Minotaur will find him. If he can kill it, the string will lead him back out."

On the night before they were sent to the Minotaur, Ariadne went secretly to the place where Theseus and the others were being held. "I loved you the moment I saw you," she whispered to Theseus. "I've come to help you. I hate these sacrifices, but my father would kill me if he learns what I've done. I'll tell you how to defeat the Minotaur if you'll promise to take me with you to Athens."

Theseus felt love fill his own heart as he listened to the king's daughter who had come to his rescue. "I will take you home as my wife if we escape," he promised.

She gave him the ball of string and told him what he had to do. They kissed, and then she slipped away.

The next morning the fourteen Athenians were led down into the Labyrinth. The heavy iron gate slammed shut behind them, leaving them in utter darkness.

Theseus told the others to stay where they were and wait for him. He tied the string to the gate and entered into the darkness.

Theseus listened intently as he inched his way along the dark tunnels. At first he heard only the sound of his own heart beating. Then he turned a corner and heard something else—the sound of a great beast breathing. The Minotaur was lying asleep in its den. Theseus thanked Athena for his good fortune—he had found the monster first. He picked up a rock, for he had no other weapon except surprise. He was able to creep close enough to leap onto the sleeping monster's back without being struck down. The Minotaur lunged awake, bellowing and roaring. The young Athenians waiting at the gate trembled in fear as they listened to the sounds of the terrible battle that followed. At last, using only the rock and his bare hands, Theseus killed the Minotaur.

Where was the ball of string? Theseus had dropped it during the struggle. He groped about frantically in the darkness—and finally his hands fell on it. He followed its trail back to his companions. Together they forced the door open and escaped, taking Ariadne with them. They ran to their ship.

On their voyage back to the mainland, they put in at an island to rest for the night. As they lay sleeping, a vision of the handsome, flowing-haired Dionysus appeared to Theseus. The god had been visiting the island and had seen them. He too had fallen in love with Ariadne. He told Theseus he wanted her for his own.

"She loves me," Theseus dared to protest. "And I love her. She saved my life."

"She will be happier and more honored as the wife of a god," Dionysus said. "Go now, and leave her with me—I command you!"

Theseus was broken-hearted, but even he dared not disobey a god—especially one as moody as Dionysus. He went back to his ship and sailed away.

When Ariadne awoke, she thought Theseus had abandoned her, and her own heart broke. But Dionysus comforted her. He gave her a beautiful diadem as a wedding present. He loved her dearly for many years, and when she died Dionysus had the crown placed in the sky as a constellation, in her memory.

Theseus sailed on, but his happiness had gone with his lost love. He was so distraught that he forgot to raise the white sail as his ship reached the harbor at Athens.

His father, watching from the city walls, saw the black sail and thought that his son had died. "I should never have let him go!" Aegeus cried. In his grief, he flung himself from the city wall into the sea below. Ever since, it has been called the Aegean Sea.

Theseus was declared the new king of Athens. He was hailed as a hero, for he had saved the people from the cruelty of the Cretan king. But he had lost his father and the woman he loved. His own painful experiences made him a wise and sympathetic leader. Theseus told his people that he did not want to be king. Instead, he set up the world's first democracy, so that the people of Athens could vote to decide their own future. He told them he would be only their commander in chief, in case of a war. Athens became a happy and prosperous city-state. All the world admired Athens and its leader. The Athenians, whose patron was the goddess of wisdom, admired Theseus most of all.

Theseus showed his wisdom and compassion in many ways over the years. He helped his cousin Hercules to recover from madness. He took in the aged, friendless King Oedipus, who had wandered the world after he had unwittingly killed his own father.

But Theseus was still a young man and loved adventure for its own sake. He took part in a battle against the Amazons and fell in love with one of the captive warrior women. Her name was Antiope, and her reluctant admiration for his skill as a warrior turned to love. He took her back to Athens with him, where they had a son named Hippolytus.

The other Amazons eventually came to rescue Antiope, because they were sure that she did not want to be in Athens. The Amazons were the only invading army ever to fight its way into the city. Although Antiope loved Theseus, the life of an Athenian woman bored and frustrated her. When she saw that her people had come for her, she realized how much she had missed her free life. She told Theseus that she wanted to return home. Reluctantly but wisely, Theseus let her go away with the Amazons. Their son stayed with him, to become the future leader of Athens.

After Theseus' old enemy, King Minos, died, the people of Athens and Crete finally made peace with each other. Theseus married Phaedra, the sister of his lost love, Ariadne, and watched over his city for many more years.

DAEDALUS
AND ICARUS

King Minos of Crete was furious when he learned that Daedalus, his architect and inventor, had helped Theseus kill the Minotaur and escape with Ariadne. As punishment he had Daedalus and his son, Icarus, shut away in a high tower. Birds were their only visitors. There seemed to be no way to escape.

Daedalus' clever mind told him that nothing was impossible, however—even that he and his son might fly away like birds. He began to pluck a few feathers from each bird that visited the tower roof. With his son's help, he constructed two pairs of wings, using candle wax to glue the feathers to a frame. Because the feathers came from many birds, the wings were all the colors of the rainbow. He made a large pair for himself and a small pair for his son. At night they practiced flying, circling above the tower roof.

"Listen well, Icarus," Daedalus said when they were ready at last to make their escape. "Follow me closely as we fly. Don't fly too low, or your wings will get wet and heavy from the sea spray. And don't fly too high, or the sun will melt the wax."

Icarus began to fall, too.

He spiraled down toward the sea and disappeared into the blue-green water.

Icarus nodded. "I promise, Father," he said. They launched themselves from the tower roof and flew off over Crete and across the Mediterranean Sea. Looking up, farmers and fisherfolk thought they were seeing gods.

And Icarus began to feel like a god. He was flying! It was the most wonderful thing he had ever known. He began to soar higher and higher, forgetting his father's warning. He ignored his father's cries as he flew ever closer to the sun.

Suddenly he saw a feather spin loose from his wing tip—and then another and another. The heat of the sun was melting his wings. Feathers fell like snow. Icarus began to fall, too. He spiraled down toward the sea and disappeared into the blue-green water. His horrified father could do nothing to save him. Heavy-hearted, Daedalus flew on alone.

At last Daedalus reached land, and safety, on the island of Sicily. The king of Sicily was glad to welcome such a distinguished inventor to his country. Daedalus designed many fine palaces and buildings there. He also made many clever toys for the king's two daughters, whose affection for him helped ease the loss of his son.

When Minos learned of Daedalus' escape, he set out with a fleet of ships to find him. Minos had a sinister trick that he was sure would show him where Daedalus was hiding. He visited one island and then another, and each time told the ruler that he would give a large reward to whoever could pass a thread through the spirals of a conch shell. He was sure that only Daedalus would be clever enough to find a way.

He was right. When he reached Sicily, the king of Sicily unsuspectingly told Daedalus of Minos' challenge. Daedalus drilled a tiny hole in the end of the conch shell. He fastened a piece of fine thread to an ant and popped it into the hole. He smeared honey on the outer edge of the shell. The ant crawled around and around through the spirals until it found the honey. Daedalus fastened a thicker thread to the fragile one and drew it through the shell. The king's servants took the threaded shell back to Minos. "Aha!" Minos said. "Daedalus is here!" He demanded that the king of Sicily hand Daedalus over. The king refused, and in the battle that followed, Minos was killed. Daedalus stayed on in Sicily, safe and happy at last.

ECHO AND NARCISSUS

Echo was a nymph and a favorite companion of Artemis. She was lively and loved to talk. Unfortunately the very thing that endeared her to her friends led her to a tragic fate.

One day Zeus slipped away from Olympus to spend the day flirting with some of the nymphs. Hera learned that he had gone down to the earth and followed angrily.

Echo saw Hera stalking through the forest, wearing a frown as dark as one of Zeus' thunderstorms. Echo knew her friends would be in terrible trouble if Hera found them dallying with Zeus. Quickly she stepped out of the trees and called to the angry goddess.

Echo began to talk about anything that came into her head. At first Hera was as amused by her gay chatter as everyone else. But every time Hera tried to leave, Echo would say something more and force Hera to answer. By the time Hera finally got free of Echo, the nymphs and Zeus had all fled to safety.

Hera, realizing she had been tricked, turned her anger on Echo. "So, you always want the last word, do you?" she snapped. "Very well. Then you shall have it. But you will never speak the first word again!"

Suddenly Echo found that she could not speak. She could only repeat someone else's words. She was so mortified that she ran away into the forest.

One day, in her forlorn wanderings, Echo saw a youth named Narcissus, who was out hunting with his companions. She had never seen anyone so beautiful. She fell instantly, hopelessly, in love with him.

Narcissus was a vain, cold young man. Women fell in love with him constantly, but he would have nothing to do with them. He felt that none of them possessed beauty equal to his own, and rejected them with cruel insults. "You aren't fit to be seen with me!" he would say, and leave them weeping.

Echo, who did not know this, followed Narcissus through the woods. She was madly in love, but too shy to reveal herself when she could not even speak to him. At last her chance came to be noticed when he heard her footsteps and called out, "Is anyone here?"

"Here! Here!" Echo repeated. "Then come!" Narcissus called impatiently. "Come!" Echo cried joyously, holding out her arms as she came through the trees toward him.

Narcissus saw that it was just one more pretty girl who was pursuing him. He frowned in disgust. "Go away!" he shouted. "You ugly thing. I would die before I let you have power over me!"

"Have power over me!" Echo cried pitifully. Her eyes filled with tears. But Narcissus turned his back on her and ran off into the woods.

Echo still followed him, hiding among the trees, unable to help herself. At last Narcissus stopped at a quiet pool to take a drink. As he knelt down by the still water, he saw his own reflection. And then Nemesis, the goddess whose name means *righteous justice*, repaid Narcissus for all his heartless cruelty.

"May he who loves no one else love only himself," she said, pointing her finger. And Narcissus, looking at his reflection, fell

As he knelt down by the still water, he saw his own reflection.

in love with it. "Alas!" he cried. "Now I know what I have done to others!" For no matter how he tried, he could not hold or caress the beautiful youth he saw in the pool. The image always fled from his touch, only to come back again to haunt him. But he could not bear to leave it, even for a moment—not even to eat. And so he sat and gazed at himself until he wasted away and died, calling one last weak word of longing—"Farewell!"—to his reflection.

Wistfully Echo answered him, "Farewell!" She crept away, hiding in caves and deep valleys, alone with her sorrow. She too wasted away, until there was nothing left of her except her voice, forlornly answering the calls of passersby.

The other nymphs, far kinder-hearted than Narcissus had ever been, pitied him and came to the pool to bury his body. But when they arrived, they found instead a new flower, a very beautiful one, blooming brightly in the grass. They named it after him—Narcissus.

HERCULES

Hercules, known as Heracles to the Greeks, was the strongest man who ever lived, and probably the most famous Greek hero of all. His mother was the princess Alcmena, a granddaughter of Perseus and Andromeda.

Hercules' father was Zeus, and so of course Hera hated both Alcmena and her newborn baby. One night Hera sent two poisonous snakes to creep into Hercules' cradle and bite him. But the baby woke, grabbed both snakes by the neck, and strangled them. When his mother rushed into his room, she found the infant happily clutching their dead bodies. Everyone knew then that Hercules would do great things someday.

As Hercules grew older, he was taught the skills that all Greek boys were expected to learn. He liked spear throwing, wrestling, and chariot driving. But he did not like his music lessons. One day in a fit of anger he hit his music tutor over the head with his lyre and killed the poor man. He was very sorry. He had not meant to do it, but he didn't know his own strength.

All his life Hercules had difficulty controlling his temper. Whenever he got angry, he got into trouble. But when his strength and lack of self-control made him do harm, he always regretted it. He wanted to make up for any wrong he had done. He was so strong that no one could have forced him to, but he always felt responsible for his acts. That is part of what made him a great man, and a hero.

Hera often got Hercules into trouble. When he was full grown, he became famous for his deeds of strength and courage.

Hera was envious and angry because Zeus bragged so about his famous son's exploits. After Hercules slew the wild beasts that had been terrorizing the countryside around Thebes, his home, Hera made him insane, to prove that he was not all-powerful. In his madness Hercules killed his own wife and children.

When he recovered and found out what he had done, Hercules was so grief-stricken that he no longer wanted to live. His wise, compassionate cousin Theseus comforted him. "You are not to blame for what you did," Theseus said. "You were out of your mind."

So Hercules went to the oracle at Delphi and asked what he must do to make up for his terrible deed. The oracle told him he had to work as a slave for his cousin King Eurystheus, and do whatever Eurystheus ordered him to do. If he could complete twelve nearly impossible tasks, he would be forgiven by the gods for his terrible crime.

Eurystheus was the clever but cowardly king of Mycenae. He had always been jealous of his famous cousin. So he thought up the most difficult tasks he could. Later these were known as the Twelve Labors of Hercules.

The first thing Eurystheus ordered Hercules to do was to kill the Nemean lion, a beast no weapon could wound. Hercules found the lion in the hills, but his arrows bounced off its hide and his club broke against it. Finally Hercules grabbed the fierce beast from behind and strangled it with his bare hands. He skinned it, and ever after wore its hide like a cape, with its head as a helmet, the fierce eyes glaring out at people from above his own.

Hercules returned to Eurystheus' city with the lion's hide. When Eurystheus saw that Hercules had actually done the deed, he was both impressed and nervous. He ordered Hercules not to come inside the city walls from then on. Eurystheus gave all his orders to Hercules while standing safely on the city's battlements.

Hercules' next task was to kill the Hydra, a many-headed monster living in a swamp near Lerna. One of the Hydra's heads was immortal—it could never be killed. Hercules attacked the Hydra with sword and club, but whenever he knocked off any of its heads, it grew two new ones. Seeing this, Hercules told his nephew Iolaus, who had come to help in the battle, to hold a torch ready. When Hercules knocked off a head, Iolaus cauterized the neck with his torch so no new head could grow. Finally only the immortal head was left. Hercules buried it under a huge boulder.

For his third labor, Hercules had to bring back a stag with golden horns that belonged to Artemis. Though Hercules could have easily killed it, Eurystheus wanted it alive. It took Hercules almost a year to capture the stag, but he brought it back alive.

Next Hercules was ordered to capture and bring back—alive—a huge boar that lived in the mountains. Shouting and banging his club on the ground, Hercules chased the boar until it was exhausted, then drove it into a snowbank and trapped it. When Hercules brought the snorting, fuming boar back to Mycenae, Eurystheus was so frightened that he leaped into a brass urn and hid there, trembling.

Even as he hid there, however, Eurystheus was busy inventing more difficult tasks for his cousin. He wanted Hercules away from his city again as quickly as possible.

The next task Hercules was sent to perform was heroic, too, in its way—although it didn't require courage. Eurystheus was annoyed that Hercules accomplished his tasks so easily. So he ordered Hercules to clean the stables of King Augeas, which had not been shoveled out in thirty years. Hercules was ordered to clean the stables in one day—something that no one could have done in a month. When Hercules arrived at the stables, he realized he needed help no human could give him. So, with straining muscles he changed the courses of two rivers that flowed nearby. Then he broke down the stable wall so that the rivers poured through the stables and swept them clean.

Eurystheus was annoyed and angry when Hercules came back the very next day, without a speck of filth on him, to report that the stables were clean. He muttered that Hercules had cheated by getting the rivers to do his work for him, and then thought long and hard to come up with a task that his cousin could not accomplish.

At last he thought he had one. He sent Hercules to chase away the man-eating Stymphalian birds. Their beaks were like spear points, and their feathers, made of brass, were as sharp as arrows. Whenever a feather dropped from their wings, it killed someone below. Because the birds lived in a marsh, Hercules could neither walk nor swim to reach them. But Athena, at Zeus' whispered request, provided Hercules with a huge rattle to shake, which frightened the birds away.

Eurystheus muttered "Unfair!" again, because Athena had helped Hercules this time. But while Hercules was gone, the king had lain awake nights thinking of ever more impossible tasks. This time he told Hercules that his daughter wanted the golden girdle of Hippolyta, the queen of the Amazons. The Amazons were a tribe of warrior women, famous for their courage and strength. There were no men in their villages—they gave away all their baby boys and kept only the girls.

When Hercules arrived at their land, even Hippolyta was impressed by his legendary deeds and strength. *Finally a man I can respect,* she thought. Hercules was equally impressed. Hippolyta told him she would gladly give him her girdle. She began to think that she might even ask him to stay and become her husband.

But while Hippolyta was talking to Hercules on his boat, Hera went to Hippolyta's warriors, posing as an Amazon. "Hercules is kidnapping your queen!" Hera shouted. The Amazons attacked Hercules and his crew. In the fierce battle that followed, Hippolyta was killed. Hercules went back to Eurystheus with the queen's golden belt and a disappointed heart.

Hercules was sent next to the land of a brutal king named Diomedes, who owned a herd of mares so fierce they would attack and tear apart all strangers. "Fetch them for me," Eurystheus ordered Hercules. Hercules threw Diomedes to his mares, and they devoured him. After the mares took their revenge, and their cruel master was dead, they let Hercules harness them to a chariot. He drove them back to Mycenae.

Next Hercules was sent to Crete, to bring back a fire-breathing bull. Zeus had given it to Minos, to prove Minos' right to be king. Minos should have sacrificed the bull in Zeus' honor, but he did not. Now the bull rampaged around the island. Even the Cretans, who had invented bullfighting, could not stop it. But Hercules was protected from the bull's fiery breath by his lion skin. He seized the bull by the horns and carried it to Mycenae on his back. Eurystheus' teeth chattered so at the sight of the bull that he could barely give Hercules his next order.

Hercules now had only three labors left to perform, but they took him farther and farther away from Mycenae. The tenth one took him all the way to what is now Spain, and beyond. He was ordered to bring back the oxen of Geryon, a monster with three heads and three bodies on a single pair of legs. Geryon lived on Erythia, an island in the western ocean (which is now called the Atlantic). On his way there from Greece, Hercules left a sign of his passing at the point where the Mediterranean Sea meets the

Atlantic. He split a mountain in half, and set half of it on each side of the entrance. These gigantic rocks, called Gibraltar (in Spain) and Ceuta (in Africa), are still known as the Pillars of Hercules.

To make the long journey to Erythia, Hercules borrowed the boat of Helios, the sun god. Using his lion skin as a sail, Hercules sailed to Geryon's island. He fought off the giant and the two-headed dog who guarded the oxen, and brought the herd back to Eurystheus.

After that, the exasperated Eurystheus literally sent Hercules to the end of the earth. This time Hercules was to bring back the golden apples of the Hesperides. The Hesperides were the daughters of Atlas the Titan, who had been forced to support the sky on his shoulders after the Titans lost their battle with the gods. No mortal knew where the Hesperides dwelled. But Atlas did, and Hercules knew where Atlas was.

On his way to find Atlas, Hercules passed the place where another Titan was still suffering a punishment inflicted on him by the gods. Prometheus, who had defied Zeus by giving mortals fire, lay chained to his rock on a mountaintop, and Hercules heard Prometheus' groans of pain as he approached. It was Hercules' custom to help anyone who might be in trouble. He was surprised to discover who lay there, and even more surprised when Prometheus said, "At last! I knew you would come some-day!"

Hercules had heard of Prometheus' legendary kindness to the human race, and of the enormous sacrifices he had made for humankind. So Hercules used his mighty strength to break Prometheus' chains and set him free. Zeus, watching from Olympus, was again impressed by his son's heroic strength.

Prometheus, filled with gratitude, offered to help Hercules in return. "I know what you are seeking," he said. "But you cannot pick the golden apples yourself. They give eternal life to the gods, but they will kill any mortal who picks them. You must ask my brother Atlas to help you."

Hercules thanked Prometheus and went on his way. He finally reached the place where Atlas stood, with the sky weighing heavily on his shoulders, and explained his errand.

"I'd be more than happy to help you," Atlas said. "But as you can see, I'm occupied."

Hercules quickly offered to hold up the sky for Atlas while Atlas fetched the apples. Atlas placed the sky carefully onto Hercules' shoulders, stretched an enormous stretch, and went to find his daughters. Hercules waited, holding up the sky.

Even Atlas' daughters could not freely give him the apples from Hera's tree: it was guarded by a dragon. Atlas had to kill the dragon. He apologized to his daughters, picked some apples, and said good-bye.

Atlas went back to where Hercules waited, supporting the sky in his place. "Why don't I carry these apples to Eurystheus for you?" Atlas said. "Then I'll come back and take the sky again."

Hercules suspected that Atlas did not intend to come back, ever. Thinking fast (which was not easy for him, especially with the sky weighing him down), Hercules said, "All right. But take the sky from me just for a moment. I want to fold up my lion skin to make a pad. This weight is hurting my shoulders."

Atlas agreed, and took the sky back. (He was apparently no mental giant himself.)

Of course, once he was free of the sky, Hercules quickly picked up the apples. He laughed and waved good-bye. "Thanks for everything," he said, and left the frowning Atlas behind.

...Atlas stood with the sky weighing heavily on his shoulders.

Eurystheus accepted the apples glumly, and hurried away to offer them to the goddess Athena. He knew she would return them to their proper place, before Hera found out and became angry.

And then Eurystheus sent Hercules off to his final labor, the most fearsome of all. He ordered Hercules to bring him Cerberus, the three-headed monster who guarded the gates of the underworld.

Boldly Hercules made his way down into Tartarus, where, with great respect, he asked Hades for permission to borrow his dog.

"All right," Hades said gruffly, because he rarely had any visitors, let alone such an interesting one. "But see that you don't hurt him."

Normally it might be expected that Cerberus, with his spiked tail and three snarling heads, would be the one to inflict any damage. But Hercules was the strongest man alive. He picked up the huge, snapping, slavering beast and squeezed the breath out of him. Then he heaved Cerberus over his shoulder and carried him up into the daylight.

When Eurystheus saw Hercules arrive at his gates carrying Cerberus, he was so terrified that he leaped back into his urn and wouldn't come out. "You're free! You're free!" he screamed. "Now go away!"

Hercules gave a sigh of relief as he felt the weight of his suffering fall from his shoulders. All that remained was to dispose of his other weight, Cerberus. He returned the hellhound to his proper home and was free at last to go on his way, without a heavy heart.

Hercules had many other remarkable adventures. One of the most famous was his wrestling match with the river god Achelous. They were competing for the hand of a lovely maiden named Deianira. Both Hercules and Achelous wanted to marry her. Deianira herself preferred the famous human hero Hercules to the slippery river god, who had the unpleasant habit of changing his shape constantly. But Achelous' shape-changing ability made him a powerful foe in a fight.

When Hercules challenged Achelous to a fight over Deianira, Achelous immediately changed himself into a raging bull. But Hercules had handled bulls before. He knew that speed was the important thing in winning this fight. He leaped on Achelous and grabbed his horns. Before Achelous could change himself into something new, Hercules had thrown him down and had torn one of the horns from his head.

This was so painful and unexpected that Achelous surrendered immediately. He melted away and flowed back into his bed to recover. Deianira and Hercules were married and lived very happily together.

But Hercules' deeds of courage often took him to distant lands far from his home. On one of his journeys he stopped at the palace of his old friends King Admetus and Queen Alcestis.

Admetus was also a friend of the god Apollo. When Apollo had heard one day that the Fates were about to clip Admetus' life thread, he asked them to change their minds. They agreed to let Admetus live a longer life. "But someone must agree to take his place," they said, "or Hades will be angry."

"I will take your place, for I love you very much," Admetus' wife, Alcestis, said, "and because I love our children, who will be safer in this hard world with their father alive than with only their mother."

Admetus did not know what to say. He watched her go with tears in his eyes, then he put on mourning clothes and wept.

When Hercules arrived, Admetus forced himself to smile and welcome his old friend. For the Greeks, being a good host—one who made guests feel welcome and safe—was considered more important than any personal feelings.

Hercules saw Admetus' mourning clothes and red eyes. He said, "Someone dear to you must have died. I won't stay."

"No, no," Admetus answered. "Please come in. It was only a distant relative." He told his servants to give Hercules a guest room at the far end of the palace, so Hercules would not be disturbed by his grieving.

Hercules, believing his host, ate much food and drank much wine. He got very drunk and sang loud, bawdy songs. The servants frowned at him and muttered, which began to annoy him. "What's the matter with you?" Hercules demanded.

"You are behaving rudely," one of the servants said. "Don't you know our queen just died?"

"What?" Hercules cried. When the servant explained, Hercules felt terrible. "I didn't know," he said. "I must make amends to my good friend." He decided the only way to do that was to bring Alcestis back to her husband.

He went down into the underworld. Cerberus whined and licked his feet as he strode through the adamantine gates to Hades' palace. "What do you want this time?" Hades said irritably. Hercules explained his quest.

Hades did not like to let people go once they were his subjects. But he was impressed by a wife who, unlike his own, loved her husband that much—and he was impressed by Hercules' boldness in coming. And Persephone, sitting coldly at Hades' side, was also moved by Hercules' story. She called Alcestis into their hall. "Go home to your children," she said. "You do not belong here. Your husband was selfish and unfair to send you here in his place." She looked at Hades. Hades looked glum, but he said nothing.

Hercules brought Alcestis back to Admetus. She hugged her husband and children.

"I made Death give her back. I hope I've made up for the unkindness I did you," Hercules said.

Admetus thanked him profusely, and the family enjoyed a long, peaceful life together, thanks to Hercules.

The rest of Hercules' life did not go as smoothly. In the end, Hercules' own beloved wife unintentionally caused his death.

Deianira had a secret potion that had been given to her by the centaur Nessus. Once, when Hercules and Deianira were traveling together, they had come to a deep river. Hercules waded across, but Deianira was afraid to follow in her long robes. Nessus, claiming to be a ferryman, offered to carry her across on his back. But when they were in midstream, the rowdy centaur began to gallop away with her. Hercules shot Nessus with an arrow, fatally wounding him.

Before he died, Nessus said to Deianira, "I'm sorry for what I did. Take some of my blood in this bottle. If your husband ever looks fondly at another woman, sprinkle it on his clothes. Then he will love only you."

Deianira saved the small bottle for many years. At last the day came when she feared that Hercules was falling in love with a beautiful princess named Iole. Deianira sprinkled the potion on an elegant man's robe and gave it to her husband as a gift.

The moment Hercules put the robe on, the potion poisoned him. Hercules roared in agony as it burned his skin, but he could not pull the robe off. The centaur had lied—this was his final revenge. When Deianira heard what had happened, she killed herself out of grief.

There was no cure for Hercules' terrible suffering, and so he, too, decided to take his own life. He asked his friends to build him a funeral pyre, high on a mountaintop. He lay down on it, as calmly as a man lying down in his bed. As his friends wept, the flames rose up around him and ended his pain.

Zeus, watching all this from Olympus, determined that the life of his heroic but troubled son should not end that way. Hercules was, after all, the son of a god. When the fire had burned away all that was mortal of Hercules, his soul rose up at last to Olympus on the billowing smoke of the pyre.

AFTERWORD

The time we know as the golden age of ancient Greek civilization occurred around 400 B.C. About three centuries later the Roman Empire spread out of what is now Italy to conquer Greece, as well as most of Europe and large parts of Asia and Africa. Though the Romans ruled over Greece, even mighty Rome admired Greek civilization and the gods its people worshiped. They "adopted" the Greek gods as their own, combining them with Roman gods, who shared many of their traits. The names of the Greek family of gods were changed, and these gods became the most important ones in the new Roman Empire. Zeus became known as Jupiter, Hera became Juno, and Demeter became Ceres. Hermes became Mercury, Aphrodite became Venus, Ares became Mars, Poseidon became Neptune, and Hades became Pluto.

Among the other Olympians, Hestia became Vesta, Dionysus became Bacchus, and Athena became Minerva. Artemis became Diana. Only her brother, Apollo, the god of light, reason, and music, did not have a Roman name. The Romans simply adopted him, complete with all his powers, calling him by his own name. The Romans were a pragmatic people, more interested in fighting wars than in the arts. As a result, Ares (Mars) was a more important and dignified figure in their mythology than he was for the Greeks. But Apollo more than any other god enlightened Roman culture with his unique and shining presence.

Centuries passed, and Rome's golden age, like Greece's, passed away. The Greeks and then the Romans had believed their gods were immortal. But even Zeus, Hera, and all their mighty family found their reign coming to an end at last, just as the

Titans' reign had ended before them. New religions flowered, and as belief in the old gods faded, so did the gods themselves. But they will never be forgotten. They live on in timeless stories just like the ones you have read here.

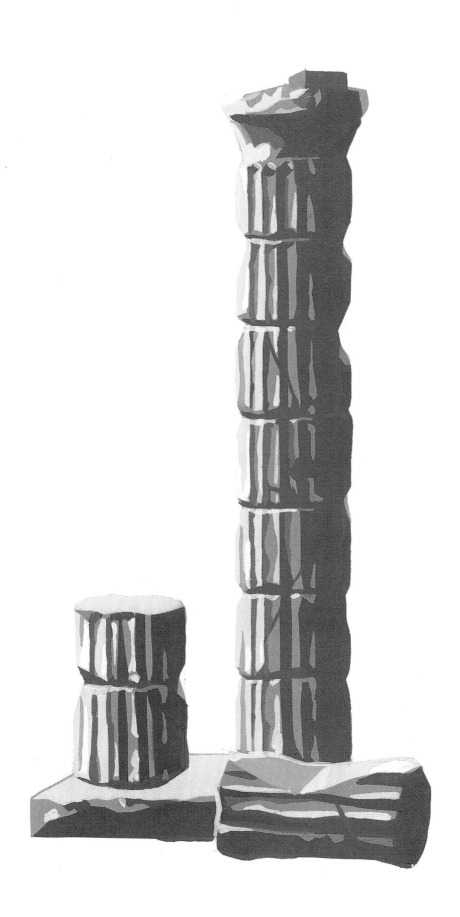

INDEX

ABOUT THE AUTHOR

JOAN D. VINGE has been called "one of the reigning queens of science fiction." She has written numerous science fiction novels, among them *The Snow Queen* and the novelette *Eyes of Amber*, both of which won the Hugo Award. Joan D. Vinge has a degree in anthropology from San Diego State University. She lives in Madison, Wisconsin, with her husband and two children.

ABOUT THE ILLUSTRATOR

OREN SHERMAN is a nationally acclaimed artist and illustrator working in the tradition of the great American poster artists of the 1920s and 1940s. A graduate of the prestigious Rhode Island School of Design, he brings his lifelong interest in and passion for Greek myths to this collection, his first foray into illustrating books for young people. Oren Sherman works in Boston's Fenway Studios and divides his time between Boston and Cape Cod.